Mademoiselle de Scudéri

D0796916

Mademoiselle
de Scudéri

A Tale of the Times of Louis XIV

E.T.A Hoffmann

Translated by Andrew Brown

ET REMOTISSIMA PROPE

100 PAGES

100 PAGES
Published by Hesperus Press Limited
4 Rickett Street, London sw6 1ru
www.hesperuspress.com

First published by Hesperus Press Limited, 2002

Introduction and English language translation © Andrew Brown, 2002
Foreword © Gilbert Adair, 2002

Designed and typeset by Fraser Muggeridge
Printed in the United Arab Emirates by Oriental Press

isbn: 1-84391-024-1

CONTENTS

One of innumerable reasons for revering Homer Simpson is that he once coined a memorably pithy definition of fiction. At the end of one episode of *The Simpsons* the family is shown mulling over the preceding plot-line in an endeavour to discern what lesson it might have held for them. Marge, Lisa and Bart having each failed to determine the story's moral, Homer, ever the bluff Johnsonian pragmatist, retorts that it had none. It was, he grunts in his inimitably uncouth fashion, 'just a bunch of stuff that happened'.

Toutes proportions gardées, Mademoiselle de Scudéri by E.T.A. Hoffmann (the 'A', incidentally, stands for 'Amadeus') is also just a bunch of stuff that happens. The novella appears to hold no lesson for us. It has no moral, no message, not even what we moderns would consider a properly developed theme, merely a plot. There is little either to be read into it or extrapolated from it. It is, in the words of a once popular, now almost wholly discredited critical refrain, a good story well told – indeed, superlatively well told.

In a sense, though, it's that which makes its status as an unimpeachable classic so very extraordinary. For just as contemporary composers are all but prohibited from writing genuine melodies, and contemporary painters from capturing recognisable likenesses, so no currently reputable author would dare, as Hoffmann did again and again – his stories number in the low thirties – to beguile his or her readers with nothing more, but equally nothing less, than an unashamed tale of the supernatural, complete with all the twists, turns, reversals and revelations one expects of the genre. These days the type of fiction of which Hoffmann was one of the most innovative practitioners, as witness the generic adjective

'Hoffmannesque', has become the virtually exclusive preserve of the purveyors of pulp.

Yet, for some reason (a reason that might merit investigation), it wasn't always so. Since his death in 1822, Hoffmann's stories have seldom been out of print, haunting and enchanting millions of readers of varying degrees of literacy. On the one hand, his work has been devoured by those who seek from fiction only the instant gratification of plot. On the other, his influence is detectable in the writings of Poe, Dickens, Melville, Gogol, Stevenson, Wilde, Chesterton, Kafka and Cortázar among countless others; and his best tales have been endlessly plundered for ballets – both Delibes's *Coppelia* and Tchaikovsky's *The Nutcracker* are Hoffmann-inspired – and operas – Offenbach's *Les Contes d'Hoffmann*, of course, in which the writer himself is the tenor lead, but also Busoni's *Die Brautwahl*, Malipiero's *I Capricci di Callot* and Hindemith's *Cardillac*, based, precisely, on *Mademoiselle de Scudéri*.

There cannot exist a single history of literature in which the invention of the detective story is not attributed to Edgar Allan Poe for *The Murders in the Rue Morgue*, which was first published in 1841. As the reader is about to learn, however, such a universally consensual presumption constitutes a major injustice, since *Mademoiselle de Scudéri*, whose publication predates that of Poe's tale by nearly a quarter of a century, is also unambiguously a detective story, seminal in more ways – ways both trivial and consequential – than one. It is, for example, the tale of a serial killer and, as such, a direct antecedent of the cannibalistic romances of Thomas Harris. And if Poe's story can legitimately claim to have been the first to boast an authentic, if amateur, detective – the unforgettable Dupin – it's worth pointing out that Mademoiselle de Scudéri, the titular character who solves the mystery at the heart of Hoffmann's, is a genteel, elderly spinster not a thousand miles away from Agatha Christie's Miss Marple.

On other, subtler levels as well, the novella foreshadows the fictions of both Poe and Christie.

One of the central thematic preoccupations of Poe's work, as of the whole sinister underside of post-Romantic literature, was that of the double – literally, in the figure of the doppel-gänger (e.g. Poe's *William Wilson*) and, metaphorically, in the pre-Freudian conception of the split personality (too many examples to list). Yet in this, too, Hoffmann, who interestingly had something of a split personality himself, toiling day after day as a respectable court official, concocting night after night some of the weirdest fantasies ever written, got there first. (To show why, I cannot avoid divulging the identity of the villain of the piece, so any reader preferring to come to the story with an 'innocent' eye is advised to turn the page now.) The real protagonist of *Mademoiselle de Scudéri* is the universally admired goldsmith Cardillac, artist by day, murderer by night, a perfectionist so perversely in thrall to his own perfection that he cannot bear to part with the exquisite artefacts in which that perfection has been invested. The artist as murderer, the intellectual as monster? As I say above, Cardillac's offspring are simply too numerous to be comprehensively listed, but one might mention Stevenson's Dr Jekyll and Mr Hyde, the fastidious poisoner Thomas Wainewright celebrated by Wilde in his essay *Pen, Pencil and Poison*, even Hannibal Lecter...

And Agatha Christie? The one thing everyone, her fans and detractors alike, knows about her whodunits is that the murderer invariably turns out to be the least likely suspect (to the point where, even if you think you've mentally fingered the least likely, Christie contrives to make it someone even less likely). It's a device which somehow feels as though it should date back no further than the interwar years of the twentieth century, the so-called Golden Age of British detective fiction. Yet, reading *Mademoiselle de Scudéri*, one is astonished to discover that Hoffmann, yet again, was a precursor, the true inventor (if one discounts the Sophocles of *Oedipus Rex*) of this classic twist, as of so much else that makes literature pleasurable.

– Gilbert Adair, 2002

The first volume of Madeleine de Scudéri's huge novel *Clélie, histoire romaine* (the whole work was published in instalments between 1654 and 1660) included the map of an imaginary country called '*Tendre*', or Tenderness. It was designed to give its readers some cartographical orientation through the difficult terrain of a love affair and to show, in particular, how the heart of a woman could be won. Setting out from '*Nouvelle Amitié*' ['New Friendship'], you might take in the town of '*Jolis Vers*' ['Pretty Poems'], en route to '*Billet Doux*' ['Love Letter'] and '*Sincérité*' ['Sincerity'], though if you deviated only slightly from your course you might find yourself successively in '*Légèreté*' ['Casualness'], and '*Oubli*' ['Forgetfulness'], possibly ending up in the '*Lac d'Indifférence*' [Lake of Indifference]. Go the opposite way, through such dubious places as '*Perfidie*' and '*Médisance*' ['Spiteful Gossip'], and you are heading straight for the stormy '*Mer d'Inimitié*' ['Sea of Enmity']. Even if you keep a straight course along the '*Rivière d'Inclination*' ['River of Inclination'], your destination may well be passionate love, but on the map this is '*Mer Dangereuse*' ['Dangerous Sea'], with, beyond it, the *terra incognita* or '*Terres Inconnues*'.

The course of true love is never easy: but Mademoiselle de Scudéri clearly did not think it necessary to include a street plan of contemporary Paris marking the places where a lover on his way to visit his mistress might run the more serious risk of being robbed and murdered. For this too, in Hoffmann's story, was one of the dangers that attended the life of love in the later years of the reign of Louis XIV. Historically speaking, Louis is associated with the triumph of a powerful, centralised monarchy over the dissipative forces that had threatened

France earlier in the seventeenth century. For this reason he has been called (by Heinrich Heine among others) the first truly modern sovereign. Artistically, he was the patron of French classicism which reached its apogee at about the same time as the events related by Hoffmann. Boileau and Racine, perhaps its supreme exponents in literature, and Claude Perrault, the designer of the east front of the Louvre, one of the clearest examples of Louis' favoured architectural style, all have walk-on parts in the story. It is to Louis the Sun-King, extolled by his courtiers as the eye that could see into every corner of his realm, that the lovers whose amorous intrigues are threatened by the spate of murders narrated by Hoffmann appeal for greater rigour in the pursuit of the malefactors. But, though set in Paris – the 'Ville Lumière' or City of Light – and nominally presided over by a king who liked to appear in his ballets as Apollo, the god of enlightenment, this is a nocturnal story whose allusions to necromancy and pacts with the devil, foreign alchemists and poisoners in thrall to strange obsessions, moving statues and hidden doors leading into shadowy backstreets, and, above all, artists of genius who are well-behaved if somewhat eccentric artisans by day but thieves and murderers after nine o'clock in the evening, all seem to drag the story into the force field of Hoffmann's own obsessions.

And yet Hoffmann did not need to import such themes: they were already there in the historical realities that formed the basis of his story. The Paris of Louis XIV was still largely a medieval place, far removed from the modern city of long rectilinear vistas and open boulevards; and the 'affair of the poisons', peaking in the 1677 trial recounted by Hoffmann, was all too real. Hoffmann describes it, early in his story, so as to establish an atmosphere of paranoia and demonstrate how even the apparently most closely knit families can conceal guilty secrets. Likewise he emphasises how, in a France that seemed to be something of a police state (albeit an ineffectual one), suspicions could attach to even the highest in the land (Racine too, though Hoffmann doesn't mention this, was named in the trial of La Voisin, the woman executed for an attempt on the King's life that involved sorcery and poison). Paris may have gone on to become a city of light, and the presiding genius of France is sometimes held to be the rationalist geometer Descartes; but Hoffmann is hardly forcing a German Romantic mould onto a story set in French classical terrain, nor does he need to look very far for the irrationality at the heart of the apparent order and decorum of Louis XIV's realm. For if Paris can appear an unusually homogeneous and centralised cityscape, it has also been the capital of surrealism, a movement that seeks out the nooks and crannies where illicit passions can flourish out of sight of those gleaming white gravel paths and dazzling perspectives. The Left Bank, source of so much of the official culture of modernity, is also home to an unusually high concentration of occult bookshops; in the late twentieth century many of the foreigners flocking to the city claimed to be there to study – just as in Hoffmann's story – magic (or, if not, another dark art: psychoanalysis). Not for nothing does the apparent gang of murderers wreaking havoc on the Paris of the Sun King call itself 'The Invisibles', able, as they seem to be, to evade his Apollinian gaze.

Hoffmann's story is sometimes hailed as the first real detective story, but if the secret of the murders is solved, it is not by any process of deduction, nor even, as is occasionally claimed, by the inner feeling of a Mademoiselle de Scudéri who is convinced in her heart that Olivier Brusson loves Madelon so deeply that he simply cannot be involved in the murders. She is wrong: he *is*, if not directly, at least by complicity. He knows that Cardillac, Madelon's father, is the murderer, but he suspects – without having the courage to put it to the test – that a public revelation of this fact would kill Madelon, even after Cardillac's own death: Brusson is prepared to go to his own execution rather than, as he sees it, betray Madelon. This decision is heroic, but condescending: it condemns Madelon to the realm of illusion that has held sway through most of the tale, and it means that the atmosphere of guilt that attaches itself to almost all the major participants is not entirely dissipated, and the secret not fully divulged, as the story ends with Brusson and Madelon going off to Geneva, she still blissfully unaware of her father's villainy. As in *King Lear*, the truth about fathers ought, surely, to be told, even if the result is catastrophic. Or rather, there are many truths about Cardillac: he is a murderer, but also a great artist; and his pathological compulsion to murder is something he has struggled against, even attempting to seek the help of the Madonna, but in vain… Perhaps these many truths, which have to be arranged in some hierarchy, would be less deadly than the bald statement 'your father is the murderer'.

Scudéri's inner feeling, meanwhile, has helped to postpone the torture of Brusson sufficiently for this guilty secret to remain undisclosed: she hopes her feeling, which again and again is shown to fly in the face of all the evidence, will somehow evoke a corresponding feeling in the King, persuading him to temper justice with mercy and give Brusson the benefit of the doubt. It does, but only just: the story foregrounds how contingent these inner feelings actually are – the King is touched by the artistry of Scudéri's pleas (it is important that she, like Cardillac, is an artist, although she uses her art more benevolently: the historical Scudéri in fact won the first prize

xiv

for eloquence awarded by the *Académie française*), but he is moved more by the beauty of Madelon, who seems to remind him of his love for La Vallière. But this in turn could easily backfire since this earlier mistress is now an austere Carmelite, reminding him perhaps of the demands of devoutness represented by his current mistress Madame de Maintenon, and hence his duty to put himself above the claims of romance. The heart is no judge of the truth: it is not surprising that, faced with this dawning realisation, Mademoiselle de Scudéri comes to despair of finding any truth at all.

The affair of the poisons, which should have taught everyone living in Paris that you can't trust even your own family members, is something she has not learnt from. Some theologians have argued that we should trust in God alone; but God is no thing or person in the world; therefore we should trust no thing or person in the world. This interesting argument seems largely endorsed by Hoffmann's story which is doubly negative in its conclusions: for if most detective stories are epistemologically optimistic (the mystery *is* solved, human powers of reasoning and deduction *can* work) while ethically pessimistic (the world encountered by the detective is darkened by crime), this one is pessimistic on both counts – if the mystery is solved, it is by a series of unusually contingent chance events and hunches. And if the faith of Scudéri is ratified, the vehicles of faith are deeply compromised: the secret entrance used by Cardillac to facilitate his murders was possibly put there by the errant monks who had used it to slip in and out of their monastery unobserved, and when much of his treasure ends up in St Eustache, it is difficult to know whether it is being thereby purged of its associations with Cardillac, or whether, on the contrary, the presentation of goods of possibly diabolical provenance to the Church does not constitute a case of simony.

The presiding type of modernity is not the saint, the prophet, or even the scientist, but the artist, and Hoffmann's artist figures are always ambiguous. The link between the art of poisoning and the art by which Cardillac not only makes his beautiful jewellery, but steals it back from his clients, goes deeper than may appear. The poison perfected by Exili and his pupils leaves no traces, just as Cardillac's apparent bourgeois rectitude acts as a cloak of invisibility. Furthermore, both the concocting of poisons and the creation of works of art is a form of alchemy, of the transmutation of base metals into gold – quite ordinary substances become a supremely potent poison, and the relatively undistinguished raw material which Cardillac is given is something he fashions into magnificent works of art. Cardillac is a driven, demonic figure, his skill indissoluble from a compulsion traceable to the prenatal influence exercised on him via his mother's fascination for a Spaniard wearing fine golden jewellery. He struggles against this compulsion in vain: the voice of the tempter is simply too strong. Is he, like another alchemist, Faust, not just demonic but diabolical – in league with the devil? Are the poisonings and murderous muggings holding Paris in thrall ultimately the work of dark spirits? The Parisians depicted by Hoffmann often resemble those of Baudelaire who, in the opening poem, 'To the Reader', of his verse collection *Les Fleurs du mal* (1857), casts a splenetic eye over the contemporary moral landscape (stupidity, error, sin, avarice) to conclude that human beings have lost the will to resist diabolical forces: 'It's the devil who holds the strings that make us move!'

One sign that the devil is in charge is the absence of authentic moral figures to act as counterweights. Here, all potential sources of legitimacy are seen as flawed. The King is vacillating, swayed by his impulses, setting up the *Chambre ardente* one minute, and regretting the power he has given it the next; the Paris mob is no less fickle; a great artist like Cardillac is a murderer; many of France's nobility and clergy are implicated in the affair of the poisons; even Mademoiselle de Scudéri allows herself hesitations and delays that threaten people's lives, and her voluminous maps of the human heart seem to give her little purchase on the intractable darkness at the heart of the established order – and, at the opposite end of the scale from her 13,000-page *Clélie*, her graceful epigram on lovers needing to have the courage of their convictions is thrown back in her face by 'The Invisibles', and made to seem like an endorsement of their murderous deeds. Even Madelon's innocence is preserved only by her being kept ignorant. Reason is overridden by the prejudice that a decent burgher cannot be guilty of murder. Art is contaminated by the ease with which it becomes criminal. If it is put into circulation (witty comments spread by the gossipy Court) it can be quoted, to devastating effect, against you; if it is withdrawn from circulation (Cardillac's jewels – can he own the labour that has gone into them and given him such fame without holding them as real artefacts in his own private museum?) it is just as dangerous. Hoffmann uses the words 'devilish' for his villains and 'angelic' for a heroine like Madelon. Perhaps the only word he really needs is 'human': for when Mademoiselle de Scudéri adjures President La Reynie to 'be human' (or 'humane' – the German word 'menschlich' can mean both), he is glad to comply, knowing that being human may include a range of behaviour, from granting mercy and pardon to – as he seems to prefer – torture.

Hoffmann's Paris, where fathers are obliged to travel long distances and cook their own food for fear of being poisoned by their children, is indeed close to the world of *King Lear*: 'Love cools, friendship falls off, brothers divide; in cities, mutinies; in countries, discord; in palaces, treason; and the bond cracked 'twixt son and father'. We may decide that 'the devil' is simply the name we give to this state of affairs: 'diabolical' just means 'the way the world is'. Or we may prefer to see this conclusion itself as the ultimate pessimism, the last temptation, with which the devil assails us, to be resisted with the (slender) hope embodied by Madeleine de Scudéri, and her frail, compromised, but still just about vindicated inner feeling.

– Andrew Brown, 2002

Note on the Text:

Hoffmann's story 'Das Fräulein von Scudéri' was first published in 1819, and then included in his sequence of *Serapionsbrüder* stories in 1820. I have used the edition *Die Serapions-Brüder. Nach dem Text der Erstausgabe, mit Nachwort und Anmerkungen*, ed. by W. Müller-Seidel (Munich, 1963). In my introduction I have ignored the interesting element of 'framing' induced by the inclusion of this story in a collection. Hoffmann drew on a variety of sources, and many of the characters and situations he refers to were real: but he conflates people and events, and telescopes history for his own ends – thus the same novel, *Clélie*, that Scudéri is supposed to be working on at the beginning of the story, in 1680, had actually been published twenty years earlier: I have largely ignored these features in my notes as they have little impact on the story as such. Mademoiselle de Scudéri's name is usually spelt 'Scudéry': I have preserved Hoffmann's spelling.

Mademoiselle
de Scudéri

In the rue St-Honoré was situated the little house which Madeleine de Scudéri, well-known for her charming poetry, lived in through the grace and favour of Louis XIV and Mme de Maintenon.[1]

Late, around midnight – it would have been in the autumn of the year 1680 – there came the sound of hard, heavy knocking at her front door, so loud it echoed through the whole hall. Baptiste, who in Mademoiselle's small household played the part of cook, lackey, and doorman all at once, had with his mistress' permission gone to the country for his sister's wedding, and so it was that Martinière, Mademoiselle's chambermaid, was the only one still awake in the house. She heard the insistent banging, and reflected that Baptiste had gone away leaving her and Mademoiselle at home quite defenceless; every crime of burglary, theft and murder ever committed in Paris came to her mind; she was certain that some great mob of brigands, tipped off about the vulnerability of the house, was rampaging out there, intent on gaining admittance and carrying out their evil intentions against her mistress, and so she remained in her room trembling and irresolute, and cursing Baptiste together with his sister's wedding. Meanwhile, blows were continuing to rain down thunderously on the door, and she seemed to hear a voice shouting out in the intervals: 'Just open up, for Christ's sake, just open up!' Finally, in increasing anxiety, Martinière quickly grabbed the candlestick with the lighted candle in it, and ran out into the hall; there she could quite clearly make out the voice of the man hammering at the door: 'For Christ's sake, just open up!'

'Now then,' thought Martinière, 'that's not how a robber talks. Who knows if it isn't someone being chased, seeking refuge with my mistress, who is always ready for any good deed. But let's be careful!' She opened a window and called down, asking who it was banging on the front door so late at night and waking everyone up: she made an effort to give her deep voice as masculine a sound as she possibly could. In the glimmer of the moon's beams breaking for a second through the thick clouds, she caught sight of a tall figure wrapped in a light-grey cloak, with a broad-brimmed hat pulled right down over his eyes. Whereupon she shouted in a loud voice, so that the man below could hear, 'Baptiste, Claude, Pierre, get up, and just come and look at this rascal trying to smash his way into our house!' But then a soft, almost plaintive voice came up to her, 'Ah! Martinière, I know it's you, my dear woman, despite all your efforts to disguise your voice, I know that Baptiste has gone to the country and that you're alone in the house with your mistress. You just need to open up to me, don't fear a thing. I absolutely must speak to your mistress, this very minute.'

'What can you be thinking of?' retorted Martinière. 'You want to speak to my mistress in the middle of the night? Don't you know she's been asleep for ages, and that I won't for anything in the world wake her from the first, sweetest slumber that at her age she really needs.'

'I know,' said the man standing below, 'I know your mistress has only just laid aside the manuscript of her novel, *Clélie*[2], that she's always working away at, and is now writing a few lines of poetry that she intends to read in the morning at the house of the Marquise de Maintenon. I entreat you, Mme Martinière, open the door to me, for pity's sake! I'm telling you it's a matter of saving an unfortunate soul from ruin, that the honour and freedom, the very life of a man depends on these few minutes in which I have to speak to your mistress. Just reflect that your lady's anger would weigh heavily on you forever if she found out it was you who had been hard-hearted enough to turn away from her door an unfortunate man who had come to beg for her help.'

'But whyever are you appealing to Mademoiselle's sympathy at *this* time of night? Come back early tomorrow,' rejoined Martinière; the man below replied in turn:

'Does fate worry about times and seasons, when it strikes like a deadly flash of lightning wreaking its havoc? Should you hesitate to offer help when it won't be possible to do so a few minutes later? Open the door for me, fear nothing from a wretched man: defenceless, abandoned by the whole world, pursued, harried by a monstrous fate, he has come to beg your mistress to rescue him from imminent danger!'

Martinière heard the man below groaning and sobbing in deep pain as he said these words; and the tone of his voice was that of a young man, soft and heart-piercing. She felt moved to the depths of her being, and without a moment's further thought she went and got the keys.

She had barely opened the door when the cloaked figure burst in and shouted wildly, pushing past Martinière into the hall, 'Lead me to your mistress!' Martinière, startled, lifted up the candlestick, and the candle's flickering light fell on the deathly pale, dreadfully contorted face of a young man. Martinière was so terrified she almost fainted when the man tore his cloak open and the shining hilt of a dagger appeared protruding from his belt. The man glared at her with flashing eyes, and shouted even more wildly than before: 'Take me to your mistress, I tell you!'

Martinière now imagined Mademoiselle in the most imminent danger; all the love she felt for her dear mistress, whom she also honoured as a pious, faithful mother, surged up more ardently within her, and induced in her a courage that even she would scarcely have believed herself capable of. She hastily slammed shut the door of her chamber, which she had left open, planted herself in front of it, and said in forceful, firm tones: 'To tell you the truth, your crazy behaviour here indoors doesn't match the pitiful words you were uttering outside: I can see all too clearly now that you were simply trying to play on my sympathy. You chose the wrong time. You cannot and will not speak to Mademoiselle now. If you're not up to mischief, and aren't afraid to show your face in broad daylight, then come back in the morning, and ask for what you want then! – and now, clear off out of the house!' The man heaved a muffled sigh, stared at Martinière with a terrible expression in his eyes, and reached for his dagger. Martinière silently commended her soul to God, but she stood steadfast, and looked the man boldly in the eye, while pressing herself more firmly against the door of the chamber through which the man would have to go to reach Mademoiselle. 'Let me in to your mistress, I tell you,' the man shouted once more. 'Do what you want,' retorted Martinière, 'I'm not budging an inch from this place, just go ahead and finish the wicked deed you've begun: you too will end up dying a shameful death on the Place de Grève, like your cursed accomplices.'

'Ha!' the man yelled. 'You're right, Martinière! I look like a damned robber and murderer, and I'm armed like one: but my accomplices aren't executed yet, oh no, not executed yet!' Whereupon, darting venomous glances, he drew his dagger on her, frightened to death as she was. 'Jesus!' she called, waiting for the fatal blow, but at that minute was heard the clatter of weapons and the clop of horses' hooves out in the street. 'The police – the police! Help, help!' cried Martinière.

'You vile woman, you want me ruined – now I've had it, I've really had it! Here! Take this; give it to your mistress today – in the morning if you want…' Softly muttering these words the man had torn the candlestick from Martinière's grasp, blown out the candle, and thrust a small casket into her hands. 'As you hope for salvation, give this casket to your mistress,' he shouted, and rushed out of the house. Martinière had slumped to the ground; she hauled herself up and felt her way back through the dark to her chamber, where in total exhaustion, unable to utter a sound, she sank into her armchair. Suddenly she heard the jingling of the keys that she had left in the lock of the front door. She heard the door being locked and hesitant steps padding towards her chamber. Spellbound and paralysed, without the strength to move a muscle, she awaited the dreadful event; but what were her feelings as the door opened and, in the gleam of the night lamp, she recognised at a glance honest Baptiste! He was looking as pale as death, and completely distraught.

'By all the saints,' he began, 'by all the saints, tell me Mme Martinière, what has happened? Ah, how worried I've been! how worried! I don't know what it was, but something forced me to come away from the wedding yesterday evening! So here I am, outside on the street. Mme Martinière, I'm thinking, is a light sleeper, she's bound to hear me if I knock nice and gentle on the front door, and she'll let me in. Then along comes this big patrol rushing up to me, horsemen there are and infantry too, armed to the teeth, and they stop me and won't let me go. But as luck will have it Desgrais is there, the police lieutenant; he knows me really well and he says, as they're holding the lantern under my nose: "Hey, Baptiste, what brings you out this way so late at night? You should be staying quietly at home like a sensible lad and keeping an eye on things. There's fishy business going on round here, and we're hoping to make a fine catch tonight." You just can't imagine, Mme Martinière, how these words set my heart racing. So I'm just stepping up to the front door, and a man wrapped in a cloak comes charging out of the house, brandishing a gleaming dagger, and runs straight into me and bowls me over – the house is open, the keys are still in the lock – tell me, what does it all mean?'

Martinière, freed of her deadly anguish, told him how it had all happened. Both she and Baptiste went into the hall, and found the candlestick on the ground where the stranger in his flight had thrown it down. 'It's all too clear,' said Baptiste, 'that our mistress was going to be robbed and probably even murdered. That man knew, as you say, that you were alone with Mademoiselle, and he even knew that she was still awake getting on with her writing; he was certainly one of those damn scoundrels and villains who get inside a house, slyly take a look around, and make a note of everything that might come in handy for their diabolical machinations. And as for the casket, Mme Martinière, that, I think, we will throw into the Seine, just where the river's at its deepest. Who's to say that some despicable fiend isn't intent on our good mistress' life: if she opens the casket she could well fall down dead, just like the old Marquis de Tournay when he opened that letter addressed to him by an unknown person!'

After long deliberation, the trusty servants finally decided to tell Mademoiselle everything the next morning, and also to hand over the mysterious casket for her to open with all due care. Both of them went over every detail of the appearance of the suspicious stranger, and came to the conclusion that some deep mystery could well be at stake, which they should not try to solve on their own initiative, but entrust to their mistress.

Baptiste's apprehensions were well-founded. At that very time Paris was the scene of the most heinous atrocities; at that very time the diabolical inventiveness of hell was managing to come up with the easiest possible means of bringing them about.

Glaser, a German apothecary, the best chemist of his time, was occupied, as specialists in his science often are, with experiments in alchemy. He had his eye on the possibility of finding the philosophers' stone. He was joined in this endeavour by an Italian named Exili. But for the latter, the art of making gold was merely a pretext. He simply wanted to learn how to mix, prepare, and sublimate the poisonous substances from which Glaser hoped to make his fortune, and he finally succeeded in concocting that subtle poison which, odourless and tasteless, can kill its victim either on the spot or else more slowly, leaves not the slightest trace in the human body, and evades all the art and science of doctors who, not suspecting murder by poison, are forced to ascribe death to natural causes. However carefully Exili went to work, however, he came under suspicion of selling poison, and was interned in the Bastille. In the same cell, Captain Godin de Sainte-Croix was shortly thereafter locked up with him. He had long been living with the Marquise de La Brinvilliers in a relationship which brought scandal on the whole family; and finally, as the Marquis de La Brinvilliers remained indifferent to the crimes of his spouse, her father, Dreux d'Aubray, Civil Lieutenant of Paris, was forced to separate the criminal couple by issuing an order for the arrest of the Captain. A hot-headed man, without any strength of character, feigning piety and inclined to vices of every sort since his youth, jealous and driven almost mad by vengeful thoughts, nothing could have been more welcome to the Captain than Exili's diabolical secret, that gave him the means of destroying all his enemies. He became Exili's assiduous pupil, and was soon on a par with his master, so that on his release from the Bastille he was in a position to carry on working by himself.

9

La Brinvilliers was a degenerate woman: thanks to Sainte-Croix she became a monster. He enabled her little by little to poison first her own father, in whose house she was living, pretending with despicable hypocrisy to be looking after him in his old age, and then both her brothers, and finally her sister; her father she murdered out of a desire for vengeance, the others so she could get her hands on their rich inheritance. The stories of several poisoners provide us with the most dreadful proof that crimes of this kind become an irresistible compulsion. Poisoners have often murdered people whose life or death was a matter of perfect indifference to them, with no further aim in view than their own sheer pleasure, in exactly the same way a chemist performs experiments for his own satisfaction. The sudden demise of several paupers in the Hôtel-Dieu later aroused the suspicion that the loaves which La Brinvilliers had been in the habit of distributing there every week, to create the impression she was a model of piety and benevolence, had been poisoned.[3] One thing is certain: she poisoned the pigeon pie that she served up to her guests. The Chevalier du Guet and several other people fell victim to these dinners from hell. Sainte-Croix, his accomplice and valet La Chaussée, and La Brinvilliers managed for a long time to conceal their horrible misdeeds behind an impenetrable veil; but however great the heinous cunning shown by such villains, the time comes when the eternal power of heaven decides to punish the evildoers already here on earth!

The poisons which Sainte-Croix concocted were so subtle that if the powder (*poudre de succession*, the Parisians called it) were exposed to the air during its preparation, a single inhalation was enough to poison you in an instant. For this reason Sainte-Croix wore a mask of fine glass while engaged in his operations. One day this mask fell off just as he was about to pour the poisonous powder he had prepared into a phial, and, breathing in the fine particles of poison, he immediately dropped down dead. As he had passed away without heirs, the lawyers hurried along to seal his estate. There they found locked away in a chest the entire hellish arsenal of poisons at the murderous disposal of the heinous Sainte-Croix; but they also discovered La Brinvilliers's letters, which left no doubt about her misdeeds. She fled to a convent in Liège. Desgrais, an officer in the mounted police, was sent after her. Disguised as a priest, he presented himself at the convent where she had gone into hiding. He managed to start up a love affair with the dreadful woman, and to lure her to a secret tryst in a solitary garden outside the town. But hardly had she arrived there than she was surrounded by Desgrais's armed men, and the priestly lover suddenly transformed himself back into a police officer, compelled her to get into the carriage that was standing waiting outside the garden, and immediately drove her off, surrounded by an escort of his men, to Paris. La Chaussée had already been beheaded; La Brinvilliers suffered the same death; her body was burnt after the execution, and the ashes scattered to the winds.

The Parisians breathed a sigh of relief now that the world was rid of this monster who had wielded his secret murder weapon against friend and foe unpunished. But it soon became known that the dreadful art of the despicable Sainte-Croix had been passed on to a successor. Like an invisible, malicious ghost, death found a way of slipping into the most tight-knit circles, such as only the ties of kinship, love, or friendship can form, and seized surely and swiftly on its unhappy victims. The man who appeared in blooming health the one day was tottering around sickly and ailing the next, and no doctor's art could save him from death. Riches, a lucrative position, a beautiful wife perhaps a bit too young for him – any of these were enough for him to be tracked down and murdered. The cruellest suspicion rent the holiest bonds asunder. The husband trembled before his wife, the father before his son, the sister before her brother. Food and wine remained untouched at the meals to which friend invited friend, and where once pleasure and merriment had reigned, people stared with wild-eyed suspicion, trying to detect a hidden murderer. Fathers were seen anxiously buying groceries in distant regions, and cooking them themselves at some dirty hot-food stall, fearful of some diabolical treachery in their own houses. And yet the most careful and most ingenious precautions were all too often unavailing.

The King, wishing to put a stop to this increasingly calamitous state of affairs, appointed a special tribunal, which he entrusted with the exclusive task of investigating and punishing these secret crimes. This was the so-called *Chambre ardente*[4], that held its sessions not far from the Bastille and was presided over by La Reynie. But La Reynie's endeavours, however assiduous, long remained fruitless, and it was left to the artful Desgrais to discover where crime was secretly lurking.

In the *faubourg* St-Germain lived an old woman called La Voisin, who occupied herself with fortune-telling and necromancy. With the help of her accomplices, Le Sage and La Vigoureux, she was able to inspire fear and amazement in people who were neither weak-minded nor superstitious. But she did more than this. A pupil of Exili, like Sainte-Croix, she knew like him how to prepare a subtle poison that left no trace, and in this way she helped dastardly sons to win early inheritances, and depraved women to get new and younger husbands. Desgrais fathomed her secret, she confessed everything, the *Chambre ardente* condemned her to death at the stake, and she was burnt on the Place de Grève. In her home they found a list of all the people who had availed themselves of her help; the result was that not only did execution follow execution, but also deep suspicion weighed on even persons of high standing. So it was believed that Cardinal Bonzy had procured from La Voisin the means of quickly disposing of all the people to whom he as Archbishop of Narbonne was obliged to pay pensions. In this way the Duchess de Bouillon and the Countess de Soissons, whose names had been found on the list, were accused of associating with the diabolical woman, and even François-Henri de Montmorency Boudebelle, Duke of Luxembourg, peer and marshal of the realm, was not spared. He too was pursued by the fearful *Chambre ardente*. He gave himself up to imprisonment in the Bastille, where the hatred of Louvois and La Reynie had him incarcerated in a gloomy cell just six feet long. Months went by before it was proved that the Duke's crime could merit no censure. He had merely once allowed Le Sage to cast his horoscope for him.

One thing is certain: blind zeal led President La Reynie to acts of violence and cruelty. The tribunal completely assumed the character of an inquisition, the slightest suspicion was sufficient to lead to brutal incarceration, and it was often left to chance to demonstrate the innocence of the person accused of a capital crime. Furthermore, La Reynie was horrid in appearance and malicious in nature, so that he soon incurred the hatred of those for whom he had been appointed avenger or protector. The Duchess de Bouillon, when interrogated by him as to whether she had seen the devil, retorted, 'I think I'm looking at him right now!'

While the blood of the guilty and the merely suspect flowed

in streams on the Place de Grève, and the poisonings finally became less and less frequent, a scourge of another sort appeared, spreading renewed consternation. A gang of thieves seemed determined to get its hands on all the jewels in town. No sooner had a piece of rich jewellery been bought than it mysteriously disappeared, however well it was guarded. But what was much more terrible, anyone who dared to carry jewels in the evening was robbed or indeed even murdered on the open streets or in the dark corridors of houses. Those who managed to escape with their lives testified that the blow of a fist to their heads had struck them down like a thunderbolt, and once they had come round, they found they had been robbed, and were lying in a quite different place from where they had been struck. The murder victims, found lying almost every morning on the streets or in the houses, all had the same fatal wound: a dagger-thrust to the heart which, in the doctors' opinion, killed so swiftly and surely that the wounded victim simply fell to the ground, unable to utter a sound. Who, in the licentious Court of Louis XIV, was not involved in some secret love affair, and did not slip off to see his beloved late at night, often carrying a rich gift with him? As if the thieves were in league with spirits, they knew exactly when something of this kind was about to happen. Often the unfortunate man never reached the house where he hoped to enjoy the pleasures of love; often he fell on the threshold, or right outside the very room of his mistress, who, horrified, would discover the bloody corpse.

In vain did d'Argenson, Minister of Police, have everyone apprehended in Paris who seemed in the least suspicious to the populace; in vain did La Reynie rant and rage and try to extort confessions; in vain were sentries and patrols strengthened: no trace of the perpetrators could be found. Only the precaution of arming yourself to the teeth, and having a lantern carried in front of you, was of any help at all, and even then there were occasions when the servant was pelted with a hail of stones and his master murdered and robbed that same instant.

It was remarkable that in spite of all the investigations carried out wherever dealing in jewels might conceivably be going on, not the smallest gem came to light; here too, the investigators drew a complete blank.

Desgrais was foaming with rage at the fact that the villains were able to evade even his cunning. Whenever he happened to be in a particular district in the city, all was peace and tranquillity there, while in the next area, where no one suspected anything amiss, the murderous robbers spied the chance of rich pickings.

Desgrais had the bright idea of creating several versions of himself, so similar to each other in gait, posture, speech, physique and facial appearance that even his own men didn't know which was the real Desgrais. Meanwhile he risked his life to eavesdrop alone in the most secret and hidden places, and followed at a distance this or that man who, on his orders, was carrying precious jewellery on him. *This* man was not attacked; so the villains were apprised of even *this* measure. Desgrais fell into despair.

One morning Desgrais came to President La Reynie, his face pale and contorted, quite beside himself. 'What's the matter, what news do you have? – Are you on their trail?' the President exclaimed on seeing him. 'Ha – my lord,' began Desgrais, stammering with rage, 'ha, my lord – last night – not far from the Louvre, the Marquis de la Fare was assaulted in my presence.'

'Heaven and earth,' exulted La Reynie joyfully, 'now we have them!'

'Oh, just listen,' broke in Desgrais with a bitter smile, 'just listen first while I tell you how it all happened. – There I was, standing outside the Louvre, hell seething in my heart as I kept a lookout for the devils that mock me. Along comes a figure, treading unsteadily and constantly looking over his shoulder, right past me but without seeing me. In the gleam of the moon I recognised the Marquis de la Fare. His appearance there came as no surprise: I knew where he was slipping off to. Hardly has he gone ten, twelve steps past me, when, as if out of the ground, a figure jumps up, strikes him down and falls on him. Without thinking, taken unawares at just the moment which might deliver the murderer into my hands, I cry out loud, and am just about to leap forward out of my hiding place and jump on him; but then I get tangled up in my cloak and trip over. I see the man hurrying away as if on the wings of the wind; I stagger to my feet, I set off after him… as I run I blow a blast on my horn… from the distance my men blow their whistles in reply… things start hotting up… the clatter of weapons, the clop of horses' hooves from every side. "Over here – over here – it's me, Desgrais, Desgrais!" I shout, so loud that my voice echoes through the streets. I can still see the man ahead of me in the bright moonlight, trying to throw me off by taking this turning and that turning; we reach the rue St-Nicaise, where his strength seems to fail him; I redouble my efforts – now he's only fifteen paces at most ahead of me…'

'You catch up with him – you grab him, your men arrive!' shouted La Reynie with flashing eyes, seizing Desgrais by the arm, as if Desgrais himself were the fleeing murderer.

'Fifteen paces,' continued Desgrais in a hollow voice, breathing heavily, 'fifteen paces ahead of me the man leaps to the side of the street into the shadows and disappears through the wall!'

'Disappears? Through the wall! – You must be mad,' exclaimed La Reynie, taking a couple of steps backwards and clapping his hands together.

'Call me,' continued Desgrais, rubbing his forehead like a man tormented by evil thoughts, 'call me, my lord, a madman if you will, a crazy ghost-seer, but it's just as I'm telling you. I'm standing petrified in front of the wall when several of my men come running up out of breath; with them is the Marquis de la Fare, who has picked himself up and has a drawn sword in his hand. We light torches, we grope up and down the wall; no trace of a door, a window, an opening. It's a sturdy stone wall adjoining a house whose residents are above the slightest suspicion. Today I examined it closely. – It's the devil himself who is making a fool of us.'

Desgrais's story spread throughout Paris. Everyone's head was filled with the sorcery, necromancy, and pacts with the devil that La Voisin, Le Vigoureux, and the infamous priest Le Sage had carried out; and as it is an innate fact of our immutable nature that our inclination to the supernatural and the marvellous surpasses all reason, people were soon convinced of nothing less than that, as Desgrais had just said out of pique, it really was the devil himself protecting the heinous villains who had sold their souls to him. You can imagine that Desgrais's story was soon extravagantly embellished in every conceivable way. An account of these events with a woodcut representing a hideous devil figure sinking into the ground in front of the terrified Desgrais was printed and sold at every street corner. This was enough to intimidate the people and even to deprive Desgrais's men of all their courage, so that they now crept through the streets at night in fear and trembling, draped with amulets and soaked in holy water.

D'Argenson could see the endeavours of the *Chambre*

ardente coming to nothing, and he went to the King asking him to appoint a new tribunal, one that would have even more extensive powers to hunt down the perpetrators and punish them. The King, convinced that he had already given too much power to the *Chambre ardente*, and shaken by the horror of the countless executions ordered by the bloodthirsty La Reynie, rejected his proposal.

Another means was chosen to provoke the King to action.

In the rooms of Mme de Maintenon, where the King was in the habit of spending much of his time in the afternoon, sometimes even working there late into the night with his ministers, a poem was handed to him in the name of all imperilled lovers, complaining that as gallantry obliged them to take a rich present to their mistresses, they were being forced to risk their lives every time. It was, the poem said, an honour and a pleasure to spill your blood for your beloved in chivalrous combat; but it was quite a different matter to be exposed to the insidious attacks of a murderer against whom no weapons were of any avail. Louis alone, the polestar of all love and gallantry, could dispel the darkness of night with the radiance of his beams, and so reveal the dark mystery that lay concealed within it. The divine hero, who had blasted all his enemies, would now again draw his victoriously flashing sword, and just as Hercules had fought the Lernaean hydra, and Theseus had fought the Minotaur, he would do battle with the terrifying monster that was devouring all love's pleasures, and darkening all joy, turning it into deep sorrow and inconsolable grief.

However serious its subject matter, the poem was not without several witty turns of phrase, especially in the depiction of how lovers slipping along their secret paths to their mistresses were devoured by anxiety, and how this anxiety already nipped in the bud all love's pleasure, and all the delights of a gallant adventure. In addition to these witticisms, the poem ended with a pompous panegyric of Louis XIV, so that the King could not fail to read the poem with evident pleasure. On reaching the end of it, he turned quickly, not raising his eyes from the paper, to La Maintenon, read the poem again, this time aloud, and then asked, with a gracious smile, what she thought of the wishes expressed by the imperilled lovers. La Maintenon, true to her serious nature and displaying her usual piety, retorted that secretive, illicit paths deserved no special protection, but that the dreadful criminals did require special measures to eradicate them. The King, dissatisfied with this indecisive answer, folded up the paper, and was about to go back to his Secretary of State, who was working in the next room, when, as he darted a glance sideways, he noticed Mademoiselle de Scudéri, who was there at the time, already seated on a small armchair not far from La Maintenon. So he strode up to her; the gracious smile that had initially been playing round his lips, only to disappear, now returned; he stood in front of the lady and, unfolding the poem again, said softly: 'The Marquise may perhaps not want anything to do with the gallantries of our gentlemen lovers, and has evaded my question by disappearing down far from illicit paths. But you, my lady, what do *you* think of this poetic supplication?'

Mlle de Scudéri rose respectfully from her armchair, a fugitive blush flew like the crimson hues of sunset over the venerable lady's pale cheeks, and she said, bowing slightly, with downcast eyes:

> '*Un amant qui craint les voleurs*
> *n'est point digne d'amour.*'[5]

The King, quite astounded at the chivalrous spirit of these few words, that completely put in the shade the whole poem with its long and tedious tirades, exclaimed with flashing eyes, 'By St Denis, you are right, my lady! No new measures that blindly strike down the innocent as well as the guilty should be allowed to shield mere cowards; let d'Argenson and La Reynie just get on with their job!'

The following morning Martinière depicted in the most vivid colours all the horrors that had befallen, as she recounted to her mistress the events of the night before, and handed over to her in fear and trembling the mysterious casket. Both she and Baptiste, who stood as white as a sheet in the corner, kneading his nightcap in his hands in anxious trepidation and almost unable to speak, begged their mistress in the most melancholy tones, and for the love of all the saints, to take the very greatest care in opening the casket. Mlle de Scudéri, weighing and testing the locked enigma in her hands, said with a smile, 'You're both seeing ghosts! I'm not rich, and there are no treasures to be found in my house that are worth committing a murder for: all this the villainous assassins out there who, as you yourselves say, have acquainted themselves with the innermost recesses of everyone's house, know as well as you and I. They are intent on my life, you say? Who could have the slightest interest in killing a person of seventy-three years of age, someone who has never persecuted anyone apart from the villains and troublemakers in her own novels, who writes mediocre poetry that can't possibly arouse anybody's envy, who will leave behind her nothing more than the estate of an old lady who sometimes went to Court and a couple of dozen nicely bound books with gold edges! And you, Martinière! However hair-raising you say that strange man looked, I still can't believe that he had any evil intentions.

'So then…!'

Martinière took three hasty steps backwards, and Baptiste sank with a muffled 'Ah!' half down to his knees, as their mistress pressed a protruding steel knob, and the lid of the casket sprang noisily open.

How amazed Mlle de Scudéri was to see a pair of golden bracelets richly adorned with jewels, and a similar necklace, lying there sparkling in front of her eyes! She took the jewellery out, and as she praised the marvellous workmanship of the necklace, Martinière ogled the rich bracelets, and exclaimed repeatedly that even the conceited Mme de Montespan did not possess such finery. 'But what is all this, whatever can it mean?' said Mlle de Scudéri. At that moment she noticed a small piece of folded paper at the bottom of the casket. She rightly surmised she would find an answer to the riddle in it. Hardly had she read what was in it than the piece of paper fell from her trembling hands. She raised her eyes eloquently to heaven and then sank, as if half fainting, back into the armchair. Horrified, Martinière and Baptiste leapt to her side. 'Oh,' she exclaimed with a voice half suffocated by tears, 'oh the insult, oh the deep humiliation! Could I ever have expected such a thing to happen to me in my old age! Have I foolishly and heedlessly done wrong, like some thoughtless young thing? – Oh God, are words uttered half in jest capable of such a dreadful interpretation? – Am I now, who have always been true to virtue and blameless in piety from childhood on, am I now to be made a party to this devilish confederacy?'

Mlle de Scudéri held her handkerchief to her eyes and wept and sobbed so bitterly that Martinière and Baptiste, quite bewildered and filled with anxiety, did not know what to do to help their kind mistress in her great distress.

Martinière had picked the fateful piece of paper up off the ground. On it she read:

Un amant qui craint les voleurs
n'est point digne d'amour.

Your wit, esteemed lady, has saved us from great persecution, we who exercise the right of the stronger against weakness and cowardice, and avail ourselves of treasures that would otherwise have been unworthily squandered. As a token of our gratitude, be so good as to accept this jewellery. It is the most precious thing that we have been able to get hold of for a long time – although you, worthy lady, should be adorned with much finer jewellery than even this! We beg you not to withdraw your friendship and your gracious remembrance of us.

– The Invisibles

'Is it possible,' exclaimed Mlle de Scudéri, once she had managed to recover a little, 'is it possible for brazen audacity and despicable mockery to be taken so far?' The sun was streaming through the bright-red silk curtains at the window, and so it happened that the diamonds lying on the table next to the open casket glinted in the reddish shimmering light. As she glanced at them, Mlle de Scudéri, horror-filled, hid her face, and ordered Martinière to get rid that instant of the dreadful jewellery to which the blood of the murder victims still clung. As soon as Martinière had hastily shut away the necklace and bracelets in the casket, she said she thought it would be most advisable to hand the jewels over to the minister of police, and tell him the whole story of the alarming visit of the young man and the handing in of the casket.

Mlle de Scudéri stood up and paced slowly and silently up and down the room, as if she were pondering what to do next. Then she ordered Baptiste to fetch a sedan chair, while she requested Martinière to dress her, as she wanted to go straight to the Marquise de Maintenon's.

She had herself taken there at precisely the time the Marquise, as Mlle de Scudéri well knew, would be alone in her rooms. The casket of jewels she took with her.

Well might the Marquise be taken aback to see Mlle de Scudéri, once the incarnation of dignity and indeed, despite her years, of amiability and grace, coming in with a pale, contorted face, and faltering steps. 'By all the saints, whatever has happened to you?' she exclaimed to the poor, anguished lady who, quite beside herself and hardly able to stand, simply tottered as fast as she could to the armchair that the Marquise pushed towards her. Once she had found her voice again, Mlle de Scudéri related what a deep, unforgivable insult the thoughtless jest she had made in reply to the supplication of the imperilled lovers had brought down on her. The Marquise, once she had heard the whole story gradually unfold, expressed the opinion that Mlle de Scudéri was taking these strange events too much to heart, that the mockery of such despicable riff-raff could never affect a pious, noble nature, and finally asked to see the jewellery.

Mlle de Scudéri gave her the opened casket, and the Marquise could not suppress a loud cry of admiration when she caught sight of the splendid jewellery. She took out the necklace and the bracelets, and walked over to the window where she alternately allowed the sunlight to play on the jewels and held the delicate golden handiwork up to her eyes, so as to get a close look at the marvellous art with which each little link

23

of the entwined chain had been worked.

Suddenly the Marquise spun round to Mlle de Scudéri and exclaimed: 'Do you know, Mademoiselle, that these bracelets and this necklace could have been worked by none other than René Cardillac?' René Cardillac was at that time the most skilled goldsmith in Paris, one of the most artistic and at the same time one of the oddest men of his age. Rather on the small side, but broad-shouldered and with a strong, muscular build, Cardillac, though in his late fifties, still had the strength and the agility of a young man. This strength, that might well have been called unusual, was attested too by his thick, curly, reddish hair and his brawny, glistening face. Had Cardillac not been known throughout Paris as the most upright and honest of men, unselfish, open, unreserved, and always ready to help, his quite peculiar gaze, darting from small, deep-set, glittering green eyes, might have made people suspect him of being secretly malevolent and spiteful. As has been said, Cardillac was the most skilful practitioner of his art, not only in Paris, but perhaps of his whole age. Intimately familiar with the nature of precious stones, he knew how to handle them and work them so that a piece of jewellery that had at first seemed not particularly attractive left Cardillac's workshop dazzling in its splendour. He would take on every commission with zealous ardour, naming a price so low that it seemed to bear no relation to the labour required. Then his work gave him no rest, day and night he could be heard hammering away in his workshop, and often, just when the work was almost complete, he would suddenly decide he did not like the shape, he was filled with doubt as to whether this or that arrangement of the jewels, this or that little link of the chain, was quite exquisite enough – and that would be sufficient pretext for him to throw the whole work back into the melting-pot and start all over again. In this way each piece of work of his emerged as a pure, unsurpassable masterpiece, that threw his customer into amazement.

But then it became practically impossible to obtain the finished piece from him. On a thousand pretexts he kept putting his customer off from week to week, from month to month. It was no use offering him twice the price for the work, he refused to take a single louis d'or over and above the agreed price. If he did finally have to yield to the insistence of his customer and hand over the piece of jewellery, he could not avoid showing every sign of the deepest frustration, and even an inner rage boiling within him. If he had to deliver a more important, exceptionally precious piece of work, perhaps worth many thousands because of the value of the jewels and the extraordinary refinement of the gold work, he was quite capable of running round and round as if out of his mind, cursing himself, his work, and everything around him. But the minute someone came running up to him, exclaiming, 'René Cardillac, couldn't you make a fine necklace for my bride', or 'bracelets for my girl', or whatever, he would suddenly stop, his narrow eyes darting a fiery glance at the man, and ask, rubbing his hands, 'So, what have you got?' The man would bring out a little case and say, 'Here are some jewels, nothing very special, pretty ordinary stuff, but in your hands...' Cardillac would not let him finish, would tear the case from his hands, take out the jewels (that really were not worth a great deal), hold them up to the light, and exclaim in delight: 'Ho ho! – ordinary stuff? – by no means! – pretty gems – splendid gems, just let me get to work on them! – and if an extra handful of louis won't set you back too much, I'll throw in another couple of little gems that will dazzle you like the lovely sun itself.' The customer would say, 'I'll leave it all to you, Master

René, and I'll pay whatever you ask!' Without making any distinctions, not caring whether his customer was a rich burgher or a distinguished courtier, Cardillac would impetuously throw his arms round his neck, and hug and kiss him, telling him he was now really happy once more, and the work would be ready in a week. He would run home as fast as his legs could carry him, dash into his workshop and start hammering away, and in a week a masterpiece would be produced. But as soon as the man who had commissioned the piece arrived, happy to pay the small sum demanded and take away the finished jewellery, Cardillac would turn morose, coarse, and defiant. 'But Master Cardillac, remember, tomorrow is my wedding day.'

'What the hell do I care about your wedding! Come and ask me again in a fortnight's time.'

'The jewellery is ready, here's the money, I have to have it.'

'And *I'm* telling you that I still have a lot of alterations to carry out on it, and I don't want to let it go today.'

'And *I'm* telling you that unless you hand over the jewellery to me fair and square – I'm quite prepared to pay double for it if need be – you'll see me turning up again straight away with d'Argenson's trusty bodyguards.'

'Very well, let Satan torment you with a hundred pairs of red-hot pincers, and hang three hundredweights on the necklace to strangle your bride!' Whereupon Cardillac would shove the jewellery into the bridegroom's breast pocket, seize him by the arm, throw him out through his studio door so violently that he would crash down the whole flight of stairs, and would laugh like the devil when, looking out of his window, he saw the poor young man holding his handkerchief to his bloody nose and limping out of the house.

It was also quite inexplicable how Cardillac would often,

in the middle of enthusiastically taking on a piece of work, suddenly implore the customer to release him from the commission he had just accepted, showing every sign of turbulent inward emotion, uttering the most overwhelming pleas, even breaking into sobs and tears, and swearing by the Blessed Virgin and all the saints. Many of the people most esteemed by King and commoners alike had in vain offered great sums to persuade Cardillac to carry out even the smallest piece of work for them. He threw himself at the King's feet and implored him for the favour of not having to work for him. Likewise he turned down every commission from Mme de Maintenon, indeed he rejected with an expression of repugnance and horror her request to manufacture a small ring adorned with the emblems of art that she was going to present to Racine.

'I would wager,' Mme de Maintenon went on to say, 'that if I were to send to Cardillac simply to find out for whom he made this piece of jewellery, he'd refuse to come, because he fears a commission and will absolutely not work for me. He has, it's true, seemed to have lost some of his fierce stubbornness recently; I hear that he's working harder than ever, and hands his work over on the spot – but still with deep ill-humour and averted eyes.' Mlle de Scudéri, who was also intent on ensuring that, if only it were possible, the jewellery should come into the hands of its rightful possessor, suggested that they should have someone tell the eccentric master immediately that they did not require him to do any work but simply to give his opinion about some jewels. The Marquise approved this idea. A messenger was sent to Cardillac, and, as if he had already been on his way, he shortly stepped into the room.

When he set eyes on Mlle de Scudéri, he seemed

embarrassed and like a man who, suddenly faced with an unexpected turn of events, forgets the demands of propriety in the heat of the moment; he first made a low and respectful bow to this worthy lady, and only then turned to the Marquise. She hastily asked him, pointing to the jewellery glittering on the table draped in dark green, whether it was his work. Cardillac hardly glanced at it and, staring the Marquise in the face, quickly stuffed bracelets and necklace into the casket next to them, and vehemently thrust it away from him. Then he spoke, an ugly smile glistening on his red face, 'Indeed, Mme la Marquise, you would have to be quite ignorant of René Cardillac's work to think for even a minute that any other goldsmith in the world could create such jewellery. Of course it's my work.'

'So tell us,' continued the Marquise, 'who you manufactured this jewellery for.'

'For no one but myself,' replied Cardillac. 'You may well,' he continued, as both Mme de Maintenon and Mlle de Scudéri gazed at him in wonder, the former full of mistrust, the latter full of anxious expectation as to how things were going to turn out, 'yes, you may well find it strange, Mme la Marquise, but that's how it is. Simply for the sake of making something beautiful did I gather together my best gems, and I worked much harder and more carefully than ever before as I was working for the sheer joy of it. A short time ago the jewellery inexplicably disappeared from my workshop.'

'Heaven be thanked!' exclaimed Mlle de Scudéri, her eyes gleaming with joy, and, springing up swiftly from her armchair with the agility of a young girl, she strode over to Cardillac and laid both hands on his shoulders. 'Take back,' she said, 'take back, Master René, the property that despicable scoundrels robbed you of.' Then she explained in detail how she had come across the jewellery. Cardillac listened to the whole story in silence, with downcast eyes. Now and again he uttered an inaudible 'Hm! – Ah! – Oh! – Ho ho!'; one moment he folded his hands behind his back, another he gently stroked his chin and cheek. When Mlle de Scudéri had finished, it was as if Cardillac were struggling with quite peculiar thoughts that had come to his mind as he listened, and as if he could not quite bring himself to carry out a decision he had reached. He rubbed his brow, he sighed, he drew his hand over his eyes, as if to wipe away the tears welling forth. Finally he seized the casket that Mlle de Scudéri was offering him, sank slowly on one knee and said: 'To you, noble and worthy lady, fate has destined this jewellery. Now for the first time I realise that as I worked on it, I was thinking of you, indeed working for you. Do not disdain to accept it from me and wear this jewellery as the best that I have made for a good long while.'

'Well, well,' replied Mlle de Scudéri, in gracefully jesting tones, 'what are you thinking of, Master René? Does it befit me at my age still to deck myself out like that with shining gems? – And how is it you are in a position to give me such an extravagantly rich present? Come now, come now, Master René, if I were as beautiful as the Marquise de Fontange and as rich, then indeed I would never let the jewellery out of my hands; but what use is that vain splendour to my withered arms, and what use is brilliant adornment to my modestly covered neck?' Cardillac had meanwhile stood up and, as if beside himself, wild-eyed, and continuing to hold the casket out to Mlle de Scudéri, said, 'Take pity on me, my lady, and take the jewellery. You won't believe what deep admiration I bear in my heart for your virtue and for your great merits! So please take my little present as an attempt to prove adequately to you my innermost convictions.'

As Mlle de Scudéri continued to hesitate, Mme de Maintenon took the casket from Cardillac's hands, saying, 'Now by Heaven, my lady, you are always going on about your age, what do you and I have to do with the years and their burden! And aren't you behaving like a coy young thing who would really like to reach out for the sweet forbidden fruit if she could only get it without lifting a finger? Don't turn down valiant Master René: accept with good grace what a thousand others could not get hold of, in spite of all their gold, their begging and pleading.'

Mme de Maintenon had meanwhile forced the casket onto Mlle de Scudéri, and now Cardillac fell to his knees – kissed Mlle de Scudéri's dress – her hands – groaned – sighed – wept – sobbed – jumped up – and ran out in wild haste, as if crazed – knocking over tables so that china and glasses clashed and smashed together.

In the greatest alarm Mlle de Scudéri exclaimed, 'For the love of all the saints, what's got into the man?' But the Marquise, in an especially jovial mood, so much so that she could indulge in a little malice usually quite foreign to her nature, uttered a peal of laughter and said, 'Now we have it, my lady, Master René is dreadfully in love with you, and is setting out to besiege your heart with rich presents, in accordance with the correct usages and long-established customs of real gallantry.' Mme de Maintenon spun out the jest, urging Mlle de Scudéri not to be too cruel to the despairing lover, and Mlle de Scudéri, giving way to her inborn fancy, was swept along by the bubbling stream of a thousand merry ideas. She expressed the opinion that, if things had come this far, once she was finally vanquished she would be unable to avoid presenting the world with the novel example of a seventy-three-year-old woman of irreproachable nobility becoming the bride of a goldsmith. Mme de Maintenon asked if she could weave the bridal crown and instruct her in the duties of a good housewife, which such a slip of a girl as she was could, of course, not know much about.

When at last Mlle de Scudéri stood up to take her leave of the Marquise, she became, in spite of all the laughter and jesting, very serious again as she glanced at the jewellery casket in her hand. She said, 'And yet, Mme la Marquise, I will never be able to use this jewellery. Whatever events have brought it here, it has been in the hands of those diabolical fellows who, as brazen as the devil, indeed probably in damned league with him, are going around robbing and murdering. I am filled with dread at the blood that seems to stick to the gleaming jewellery. And now even Cardillac's behaviour, I must confess, strikes me as having something strangely apprehensive and uncanny about it. I cannot ward off a dark presentiment that some horrible, dreadful mystery is lurking behind all this, and even if I try to see things as clearly as I can, weighing up every circumstance, I still cannot even guess at the nature of the mystery; above all, I have no idea how honest, valiant Master René, the model of a good, pious burgher, can possibly have anything to do with anything wicked and damnable. This much is certain, however: I will never have the audacity to wear the jewellery.'

The Marquise thought this was taking scruples too far; but when Mlle de Scudéri asked her on her conscience what she would do if she were in *her* situation, she replied seriously and firmly, 'I'd much sooner throw the jewellery into the Seine than ever wear it.'

The scene with Master René inspired Mlle de Scudéri with some quite delightful poetry that she read to the King in the chambers of Mme de Maintenon the following evening. It is doubtless true that, overcoming the terror her uncanny presentiments filled her with, she managed to paint a splendid and delightfully vivid picture, at Master René's expense, of herself as the goldsmith's seventy-three-year-old bride of age-old nobility. It was enough to make the King laugh long and loud, and swear that Boileau-Despréaux[6] had met his match, which is why Mlle de Scudéri's poem was judged to be the wittiest that had ever been written.

Several months had gone by when chance would have it that Mlle de Scudéri was driving in the glass coach of the Duchess de Montausier over the Pont Neuf. The invention of these dainty glass coaches was still so recent that the inquisitive populace thronged the streets whenever a magnificent cavalcade of this kind appeared. So it came about that a gaping mob surrounded Mme de Montausier's coach on the Pont Neuf and almost prevented the horses from taking a step forward. Mlle de Scudéri suddenly heard a cursing and a scolding and saw a man fighting his way, his fists flailing and his elbows jabbing people in the ribs, through the densest part of the crowd. And when he got nearer, she was transfixed by the piercing eyes of a young man's deathly pale, distraught face. The young man fixed her with a steadfast gaze, as he worked away with his sprightly fists and elbows, until he reached the door of the coach; he tore it open with tempestuous haste, flung a note into Mlle de Scudéri's lap, and, doling out and receiving punches and elbow-digs, disappeared just as he had come. With a cry of horror, Martinière, who was with Mlle de Scudéri, had, as soon as the man appeared at the coach door, sunk lifeless back into the cushions. In vain did Mlle de Scudéri pull at the cord, and call out to the coach-driver; he, as if driven by the Evil Spirit, whipped up his horses, and they, foam spraying from their mouths, lashed out, reared up, and finally at a sharp gallop thundered over the bridge. Mlle de Scudéri poured her bottle of smelling salts over the fainting woman, who finally opened her eyes and, trembling and shaking, clinging convulsively to her mistress, showing dread and horror in her pale face, groaned out with an effort, 'By the Blessed Virgin! Whatever did that fearful man want? – Ah! he was the one, yes he was the one, the very same one who brought you the casket that dreadful night!' Mlle de Scudéri calmed the poor woman down, telling her that absolutely nothing untoward had happened, and that it was now just a question of finding out what was written in the note. She opened the piece of paper and found these words:

A terrible fate, one that you can avert, is driving me to the abyss! – I entreat you, as a son would entreat a mother he cannot abandon, in the fullest glow of a child's love: find any pretext at all – pretend that something needs to be improved or altered in it – and get the necklace and the bracelets that you received from me back to Master René Cardillac; your well-being, your very life depends upon it. Unless you do it by the day after tomorrow, I shall force my way into your apartment and kill myself in front of your very eyes!

'Now it's certain,' said Mlle de Scudéri once she had read it, 'that even if this mysterious man really does belong to that gang of despicable thieves and robbers, he isn't harbouring any evil intentions against me. If he had succeeded in speaking to me on that fateful night, who knows what strange event, what dark set of circumstances would have become clear to me, which in my heart I am now trying in vain to understand. Whatever the situation may be, what I am requested to do in this note I will do, even if this merely means getting rid of the wretched jewellery that I think must be a hellish talisman of the Evil One himself. Cardillac will now at least, no doubt, be faithful to his old habits and wait a long time before letting it out of his hands again.'

Mlle de Scudéri decided to take herself to the goldsmith's with the jewellery the very next day. But it was as if all the men and women of wit in Paris had arranged on that very morning to besiege her with poems, plays, and anecdotes. Hardly had Chapelle ended the scene of a tragedy, and slyly assured everyone that he was now intent on beating Racine, when the latter himself walked in, and quite outdid him with the pathos-filled speech of some king, until Boileau sent up his flares into the dark sky of the tragedies, so as not to have to listen to endless chatter about the colonnade of the Louvre, which the architecturally-inclined Dr Perrault had cornered him into.[7]

It was high noon; Mlle de Scudéri had to go to the Duchess de Montausier's, and so her visit to Master René was put off until the following day.

Mlle de Scudéri felt tormented by a strange unrest. In her mind's eye she continually saw the young man standing before her, and she tried to summon up a dark memory from her innermost being, for it was as if she had already seen that face, those features, somewhere before. Her lightest slumber was disturbed by anxious dreams; it seemed to her that she had thoughtlessly, indeed criminally hesitated to extend a helping hand to the unhappy man, sinking into the abyss and stretching out to her; as if, indeed, it had been up to her to put a stop to some dreadful event, some frightful crime! – As soon as morning had come, she had herself dressed and drove to the goldsmith's, taking the casket with her.

A crowd of people was streaming to the rue St-Nicaise, where Cardillac lived; they were gathering outside his front door, shouting and raging in uproar; they wanted to storm the door, but were held back with difficulty by the constables surrounding the house. In the wild, confused din, angry voices were shouting: 'Tear him to pieces, break his bones, the accursed murderer!' Finally Desgrais appeared with a numerous party, who forced a passage through the thickest throng. The front door sprang open, a man loaded with chains was brought out and dragged away under the most terrible curses of the enraged mob. – At the same moment that Mlle de Scudéri, half dead from terror and fearful premonitions, saw all this, a ringing cry of distress pierced her ears. 'Keep going! – keep going!' she shouted, quite beside herself, to the coachman, who with a skilful, rapid turn managed to scatter the thick throng and halted right in front of Cardillac's front door. There Mlle de Scudéri saw Desgrais, and at his feet a young girl, as beautiful as the day, with her hair let down, half undressed, wild anguish and inconsolable despair on her face, clinging to his knees and crying out in the tones of the most dreadful, most piercing agony: 'He's innocent! – he's innocent!' In vain were Desgrais's efforts and those of his men to pull her away and lift her to her feet. A strong, rough fellow finally seized her arms in his great hands, heaved her violently away from Desgrais, stumbled clumsily, and let the girl go – she rolled heavily down the stone steps and, without a noise, remained lying as if dead on the street. Mlle de Scudéri could no longer restrain herself. 'In Christ's name, what's happened, what's going on here?' she shouted, quickly opening her coach door, and climbing out. The crowd respectfully made way for the worthy lady, who, seeing that a couple of sympathetic women had lifted the girl up and set her on the steps, where they rubbed her brow with strong spirits, went up to Desgrais and vehemently repeated her question. 'Something dreadful has happened,' said Desgrais. 'René Cardillac was found this morning stabbed to death. His apprentice Olivier Brusson is the murderer. He's just been taken off to jail.'

'And the girl –?' exclaimed Mlle de Scudéri.

'– is,' broke in Desgrais, 'Madelon, Cardillac's daughter. That wicked man was her lover. Now she's weeping and howling, and shouting again and again that Olivier is innocent, completely innocent. But she well knows the facts of the case and I have to take her to the Conciergerie[8] too.' As he spoke, Desgrais darted a malicious, gloating glance at the girl; seeing it, Mlle de Scudéri trembled. The girl was just starting to breathe faintly, but she was incapable of sound or movement, and lay there with her eyes closed; nobody knew what to do, whether to take her into the house, or stay by her side a while longer until she woke up. Deeply moved, tears in her eyes, Mlle de Scudéri gazed at the innocent angel; she felt frightened by Desgrais and his men. Then there was a muffled thumping down the staircase; they were bringing out Cardillac's corpse. Coming to a rapid decision, Mlle de Scudéri loudly called out, 'I'll take the girl with me; you can take care of the rest, Desgrais!' A muted murmur of approval ran through the crowd. The women lifted the girl up, everyone pressed forward, a hundred hands busied themselves with helping them, and as if hovering in the air the girl was carried to the coach, while blessings on the old lady who had rescued innocence from a murder charge streamed forth from everyone's lips.

The efforts of Séron, the most famous doctor in Paris, finally succeeded in bringing Madelon, who had lain for hours in a rigid coma, back to consciousness. Mlle de Scudéri completed what the doctor had begun, filling the girl's soul with many gentle rays of hope, until a violent flood of tears bursting from her eyes brought her relief. She was able, although every so often her words were choked in deep sobs by the terrible distress overwhelming her, to relate everything that had happened.

Around midnight she had been awoken by a light knocking at the door of her room, and had heard the voice of Olivier entreating her to get up immediately, as her father was dying. She had leapt up in horror and opened the door. Olivier, with a pale and contorted face, dripping with sweat, had staggered to the workshop, a light in his hand, and she had followed him. There her father lay, with staring eyes, in the throes of death. She had rushed over to him uttering lamentations, and only then did she notice his bloody shirt. Olivier had gently pulled her away and then set about washing with balsam and bandaging a wound on the left side of her father's chest. Meanwhile, her father had regained consciousness, he had stopped groaning and had gazed first at her and then at Olivier with a soulful expression; he seized her hand, placed it in Olivier's, and pressed both of them vehemently. She and Olivier had both fallen to their knees at her father's bedside; he had pulled himself upright with a piercing cry, but then had immediately fallen back again and, with a deep sigh, passed away. They had both thereupon broken into loud sobbing and lamenting. Olivier had recounted how his master had been murdered in his presence while he, Olivier, had been accompanying him at his request on a night-time errand, and how he had managed, albeit with the greatest exertions, to carry the heavy man, whom he did not think was fatally wounded, back home. As soon as the new day dawned, the occupants of the house, alarmed by the hubbub, the loud weeping and wailing in the middle of the night, came upstairs and found them, still inconsolable, kneeling by her father's body. Then the news got round; the constables rushed in and dragged Olivier off to prison as the murderer of his master. Madelon now continued with the most touching depiction of the virtue, the piety and the faithfulness of her beloved Olivier. She told how greatly he had revered his master, as much as if he had been his own father; how the latter had fully reciprocated his love, choosing him as his son-in-law in spite of his poverty, as his skill had matched his faithfulness and his nobility of disposition. Madelon related all this from the depths of her heart and concluded by saying that even if Olivier had plunged the dagger into her father's breast in her very presence, she would have viewed this as a trick of Satan's rather than believe that Olivier could be capable of such a cruel and terrible crime.

Mlle de Scudéri, deeply moved by Madelon's inexpressible suffering and perfectly inclined to view poor Olivier as innocent, made enquiries, and found everything that Madelon had recounted concerning the domestic relations between the master and his apprentice to be completely confirmed. The other occupants of the house, and the neighbours, praised Olivier as the very model of decency, piety, faithfulness, and diligence; no one had a bad word to say about him – and yet, as soon as the grisly deed was mentioned, everyone shrugged and said there was something incomprehensible about it.

Olivier, brought before the *Chambre ardente*, denied with the greatest steadfastness and the most candid honesty the crime he was accused of, as Mlle de Scudéri heard; he maintained that his master had been attacked and struck down before his eyes in the street, and that he had dragged him home still alive, where he soon died. This too agreed with Madelon's story.

Again and again Mlle de Scudéri had the tiniest details of

the dreadful event repeated to her. She enquired closely whether at any time there had been a quarrel between master and apprentice, whether perhaps Olivier was not entirely free of that violent temper which often like a fit of blind madness overcomes the most good-natured people, and leads them to commit deeds that seem to override their free will. But the more forcefully Madelon spoke of the tranquil domestic happiness in which the three of them had lived together in the deepest mutual affection, the more every shadow of suspicion against Olivier, now accused of a capital crime, vanished. Weighing up everything exactly, starting from the assumption that Olivier, in spite of everything that spoke loud and clear in favour of his innocence, was nonetheless Cardillac's murderer, Mlle de Scudéri found in the whole realm of possibility no motive for a terrible deed that at all events was bound to destroy Olivier's happiness. – He is poor, but skilled, she thought. – He manages to win the favour of the most famous of masters, whose daughter he falls in love with; the master looks kindly on his suit; lifelong happiness and prosperity are his for the asking! – And even if, provoked for God knows what reason, Olivier had been overcome by anger, and laid murderous hands on his benefactor, his father, what diabolical hypocrisy there was in his behaving the way he did after the deed! Firmly convinced of Olivier's innocence, Mlle de Scudéri took the decision to save the innocent youth at all costs.

It seemed to her most advisable, before perhaps appealing to the King himself for mercy, to turn to President La Reynie, drawing his attention to all the circumstances that were bound to speak in favour of Olivier's innocence, and so perhaps awakening in the President's soul an inner conviction inclining him towards the accused – a conviction that would communicate itself to the judges, with beneficial results.

La Reynie received Mlle de Scudéri with the marks of high esteem to which the worthy lady, greatly honoured by the King himself, could justifiably lay claim. He listened calmly to everything that she had to tell him about the dreadful deed, and about Olivier's relations and character. A faint, almost malicious smile was the only sign, meanwhile, that demonstrated that her assertions and pleadings, accompanied by floods of tears, were not falling on entirely deaf ears, as she urged that no judge should be swayed by hostility to the accused, but should pay all due attention to everything that spoke in his favour.

When Mlle de Scudéri finally fell silent, quite exhausted, and wiping the tears away from her eyes, La Reynie began, 'It is quite in keeping with your excellent heart, my lady, that, moved by the tears of a young girl in love, you should believe everything she claims, and indeed be quite incapable of grasping the thought of a terrible crime like this; but it is quite different for the judge, who is used to having to unmask arrant hypocrisy. It simply cannot be part of my office to expound on the course of a criminal trial to everyone who asks me. I do my duty, my lady, and care little for the world's opinion. Evildoers should tremble before the *Chambre ardente*, which knows of no punishment except blood and fire. But I would not wish you, esteemed lady, to think of me as a monster of harshness and cruelty, and so allow me briefly and clearly to set out before your eyes the guilt of this young murderer on whom, thank heavens! vengeance has fallen. Your acute intelligence will then itself pour scorn on the kindness of heart that does you honour, but would be quite out of place in me. So: one morning, René Cardillac is discovered stabbed to death. There is no one near him apart from his apprentice Olivier

Brusson and his daughter. In Olivier's room, among other things, a dagger is found covered with fresh blood, and exactly fitting the wound. Olivier says, "Cardillac was struck down last night before my very eyes." – "Was someone trying to rob him?" – "I don't know!" – "You were walking along with him, and you didn't manage to ward off the murderer? Or grab hold of him? Or call for help?" – "The master was walking fifteen, maybe twenty paces ahead of me, and I was following behind him." – "Why on earth were you so far behind?" – "The master wanted it that way." – "And what, after all, was Master Cardillac doing out so late on the streets?" – "That I can't say." – "And yet he had never on any other occasion left his house later than nine o'clock in the evening?" – At this point Olivier falters, he is overcome by consternation, he sighs, he sheds tears, he swears by all that is holy that Cardillac had really gone out that night and met his death. Now listen carefully, my lady. It is proven beyond the slightest doubt that Cardillac never left his house that night, and consequently Olivier's assertion that he really went out with him is a blatant lie. The front door has a heavy lock which makes a grating noise every time anyone opens or closes it, and then the door creaks and groans horribly on its hinges so that, as tests we have carried out have demonstrated, the din echoes up to the top floor of the house. Now on the ground floor, that is, right next to the front door, lives old Master Claude Patru with his housekeeper, a person of nearly eighty, but still hale and hearty. Both these people heard how Cardillac, as was his wont, came downstairs at precisely nine o'clock that evening, locked and bolted the door with a great deal of noise, went back upstairs, read the evening prayers aloud, and then, as they could hear by the sound of the door closing, went into his bedroom. Master Claude suffers from insomnia, as often happens with elderly people. That night too, he couldn't close his eyes. So the housekeeper – it must have been around half past nine – went through the hall to the kitchen, lit a candle, and sat at Master Claude's table reading an old chronicle, while the old man, lost in his own thoughts, sat down one moment in his armchair, only to get up again the next moment and, trying to make himself feel tired and sleepy, walked slowly and quietly up and down his room. Everything remained calm and peaceful until midnight. Then she heard heavy footsteps overhead, a loud thump, as if a heavy burden had fallen to the floor, and immediately afterwards a muffled groaning. Both were overwhelmed by a strange anxiety and trepidation. A shudder went through them at the dreadful deed that had just been committed. – When morning came, what had been done in darkness came to light.'

'But,' Mlle de Scudéri interrupted him, 'but by all the saints, can you really, given all the detailed circumstances I've just described, imagine any motive for this hellish deed?'

'Hm,' replied La Reynie, 'Cardillac wasn't poor – he possessed some excellent gemstones.'

'But,' pursued Mlle de Scudéri, 'wouldn't the daughter inherit all that? You're forgetting that Olivier was to be Cardillac's son-in-law.'

'Perhaps he was supposed to share the spoils, or even simply carry out the murder on behalf of others,' said La Reynie.

'Share the spoils, murder on behalf of others?' asked Mlle de Scudéri in the greatest astonishment.

'You must know, my lady,' the President continued, 'that Olivier would long ago have paid with his life on the Place de Grève were it not for the fact that his crime is somehow linked to the impenetrable mystery that has been hanging so

42

menacingly over the whole of Paris up till now. Olivier evidently belongs to that cursed gang that has managed to get away with its little escapades undetected and unpunished, making a mockery of all the vigilance, all the efforts and all the investigations of the lawcourts. Through him everything will and must be made clear. Cardillac's wound is identical to those inflicted on all those who were murdered and robbed in the streets or in their houses. But the most decisive thing of all is this: ever since the time of Olivier Brusson's arrest, all the murders and all the robberies have ceased. The streets are as safe at night as they are in the daytime. This is proof enough that Olivier was perhaps even the head of that gang of murderers. He still refuses to confess, but there are means of making him talk against his will.'

'And Madelon,' exclaimed Mlle de Scudéri, 'and Madelon, the faithful, innocent dove?'

'Ah,' said La Reynie with a poisonous smile, 'ah, who can guarantee that she's not involved in the plot too? What does she care about her father? Her tears are all for that murderous boy.'

'What are you saying?' cried Mlle de Scudéri. 'It can't be possible. Her father! That girl!'

'Oh,' continued La Reynie, 'oh! Just think of La Brinvilliers! You will have to forgive me if I see myself obliged before very long to tear your protégée away from you and throw her into the Conciergerie.'

A shudder ran through Mlle de Scudéri at this terrible suspicion. She felt as if no faithfulness or virtue could survive the scrutiny of this dreadful man, as if he could spy murder and guilt in even the deepest, most hidden thoughts. She stood up. 'Be human,' was the only thing that she could utter, filled with apprehension as she was and breathing with difficulty. As she was just about to go down the stairs to which the President had with ceremonial politeness accompanied her, a strange thought came to her, she didn't quite know how. 'Might I be allowed to see the unfortunate Olivier Brusson?' she asked, turning suddenly to the President. He gazed at her doubtfully for a while, then his face crumpled into that repellent smile that was characteristic of him. 'To be sure,' he said, 'to be sure, my honoured lady; you now want to test out Olivier's guilt or innocence for yourself, trusting in your feelings and your own inner voice more than in what has happened before our very eyes. If you do not shrink from entering the dismal dwelling-place of crime, if you are not appalled by the images of every degree of depravity, then the gates of the Conciergerie will be opened to you in two hours' time. Olivier, whose fate arouses your sympathy, will be brought before you.'

It was true: Mlle de Scudéri could not convince herself of the young man's guilt. Everything spoke against him, and no judge in the world would have acted any differently from La Reynie, given such conclusive evidence. But the picture of domestic happiness that Madelon had so vividly painted for her outshone every lurking suspicion, and so she preferred to accept that there was some inexplicable mystery at work here rather than believe something that her whole inner being rebelled against.

She planned to make Olivier tell her once again all that had happened on that fateful night, so she could throw as much light as possible on a mystery that remained impenetrable to the judges for the simple reason that they had deemed it not worth bothering their heads any further about it.

When Mlle de Scudéri had arrived in the Conciergerie, she was led into a spacious, well-lit room. Not long afterwards she heard the rattle of chains. Olivier Brusson was brought in. But the minute he stepped through the door, Mlle de Scudéri fell in a faint. By the time she had come round, Olivier had disappeared. She vehemently implored them to take her to her carriage; she wanted to flee, to flee this very minute from the halls of loathsome crime. Ah! – at the first glance she had recognised Olivier Brusson as the young man who on the Pont Neuf had thrown that piece of paper into her carriage, who had brought her the casket with the jewels. Now every doubt had been vanquished, and La Reynie's dreadful supposition confirmed. Olivier Brusson belonged to the dreadful gang of murderers; he had certainly also murdered his master! – And Madelon? Never before had she been so deceived by her inner feelings; she felt harrowed to death by that hellish power on earth whose existence she had not believed in: Mlle de Scudéri despaired of all truth. She now entertained the terrible suspicion that Madelon might be one of the conspirators, capable of participating in the bloody murder. The human mind tends, once some image has fastened on it, to seek and find ever more garish colours in which to deck it out, and Mlle de Scudéri, weighing up every circumstance in the case, and going over Madelon's behaviour in the closest detail, found plenty to nourish her suspicions. So it was that many of the things that had up until now struck her as proofs of innocence and purity now seemed like definite proof of wanton wickedness and studied hypocrisy. Those heartbreaking laments, those bitter tears could after all have been induced by the mortal dread, not so much of seeing her beloved suffer death, as rather of herself falling into the executioner's hands. Mlle de Scudéri simply had, as soon as possible, to tear away the snake gnawing at her heart; this was the decision she arrived at as she stepped out of her carriage. She went into her chambers, where Madelon flung herself at her feet and, raising her celestial eyes – as faithful and true as those of any of God's angels – to Mlle de Scudéri, and folding her hands before her heaving breast, she loudly lamented and implored her help and consolation. Mlle de Scudéri made an effort to compose herself and said, trying to put as much gravity and calm into her voice as she possibly could, 'Go now – go: you will simply have to console yourself for the death of the murderer who can expect a just punishment for his disgraceful deeds. May the Blessed Virgin avert any guilt from weighing on your own head also!'

'Ah, now all is lost!' With this piercing wail Madelon collapsed unconscious to the ground. Mlle de Scudéri entrusted Martinière with the task of caring for the girl, and withdrew to another room.

Inwardly torn apart, alienated from all earthly life, Mlle de Scudéri had no more desire to live in a world full of hellish delusion. She accused destiny for the bitter irony with which it had granted her so many years of life to reinforce her belief in virtue and faithfulness, only to destroy, now that she was an old woman, the beautiful image that had shed its light on her whole life.

She could hear Martinière leading away Madelon, who was softly sighing and lamenting, 'Ah…! Even *she*… even *she* has been bewitched by those cruel men… How wretched I am… and poor, unhappy Olivier!' Her tones pierced Mlle de Scudéri's heart, and again the premonition of a mystery, and the belief in Olivier's innocence, stirred deep within her. Oppressed by the most conflicting feelings, and quite beside herself, Mlle de Scudéri exclaimed, 'What spirit of hell has entangled me in this dreadful story that will cost me my life!'

At this moment, Baptiste came in, pale and distraught, with

the news that Desgrais was outside. Ever since the abominable trial of La Voisin, Desgrais's arrival in any home had been the certain harbinger of a criminal accusation – hence Baptiste's fright. So Mlle de Scudéri asked him, with a gentle smile: 'What's the matter, Baptiste? So the name Scudéri has been found on La Voisin's list, has it?'

'Ah, for heaven's sake,' replied Baptiste, trembling in every limb, 'how can you say such a thing? But Desgrais, that terrible man Desgrais, is behaving so mysteriously, so urgently, and seems so very impatient to see you!'

'Well,' said Mlle de Scudéri, 'well, Baptiste, just lead him in right away, that man who seems so terrible to you, but in *me* at least arouses no anxiety at all.'

'President La Reynie,' said Desgrais as he stepped into the room, 'President La Reynie has sent me to you, my lady, with a request which he could not possibly expect to see granted if he were unacquainted with your virtue and your courage, and if our last hope of bringing a dreadful and bloody crime to light did not lie with you – for you yourself have already been an active participant in the awful trial which is keeping the *Chambre ardente* and indeed all of us in suspense. Olivier Brusson, ever since seeing you, has been half crazed. He at first seemed to be coming round to making a confession, but now he is again swearing by Christ and all his saints that he is perfectly innocent of the murder of Cardillac, although he is quite prepared to suffer the death that he has deserved. Note, my lady, that these last words of his obviously allude to other crimes weighing on his conscience. But all the effort to get just one more word out of him has been in vain, and even the threat of torture has proved fruitless. He is imploring and beseeching us to arrange for him to speak to you, to *you* alone; to *you* and no one else will he confess everything. Please, my lady, deign to hear Brusson's confession.'

'What!' exclaimed Mlle de Scudéri, indignantly. 'Am I to be the tool of a bloody assizes, am I to abuse a young man's trust and bring him to the scaffold? No, Desgrais! Even if Brusson were the most despicable murderer, I could never find it in myself to deceive him in such a dishonourable way. I refuse to hear any of his secrets, which, as in the sacrament of confession, would remain locked within my heart.'

'Perhaps,' retorted Desgrais with a thin-lipped smile, 'perhaps, my lady, you will change your mind once you have heard Brusson speak. Didn't you yourself beg the President to be human? That's what he is trying to be in yielding to Brusson's foolish demand, and thus making one last attempt before sentencing Brusson to the torture he has so long deserved.' Mlle de Scudéri gave an involuntary start. 'Look,' continued Desgrais, 'look, honoured lady, no one will expect you to step once more into those dark halls which fill you with horror and revulsion. In the silence of night, without any fuss or to-do, Olivier Brusson will be brought to you in your own house as if he were a free man. Then, without being overheard – although still under guard – he will be able to confess everything to you without constraint. That you have nothing to fear for yourself from the wretched man is something I will guarantee with my own life. He speaks of you with the most fervent admiration. He swears that only the dark destiny that prevented him from seeing you earlier has brought him to death's door. And then of course you are free to tell us as much as you want to of whatever Brusson discloses to you. Can we force you to do any more?'

Mlle de Scudéri stood gazing at the floor, deep in thought. She felt as if she must obey the higher power that was demanding that she clear up some dreadful mystery, and as if she could no longer escape from the incredible tangle of events in which she had unwillingly become caught up. Coming to a sudden decision, she said with dignity, 'God will give me resolution and steadfastness; bring Brusson here, I will speak to him.'

So, just as once Brusson had brought the casket, there came a midnight knocking at Mlle de Scudéri's front door. Baptiste, forewarned of the nocturnal visit, opened the door. An icy shudder ran through Mlle de Scudéri as she perceived from the light steps and the muffled murmurs that the guards who had brought Brusson were fanning out to take up their positions in the house's various corridors.

Finally the door of her room slowly opened. Desgrais stepped in, followed by Olivier Brusson, freed from his chains and decently dressed. 'Here,' said Desgrais with a deferential bow, 'here is Brusson, my honoured lady!', and he left the room.

Brusson fell to his knees in front of Mlle de Scudéri, and lifted his folded hands to her in supplication, as tears poured from his eyes.

Mlle de Scudéri, turning pale, unable to speak a word, gazed down at him. Even through features distorted by grief and despair, there shone on the young man's face the clear expression of a pure and honest nature. The longer Mlle de Scudéri allowed her eyes to rest on Brusson's face, the more vividly there sprang to her mind the memory of some person dear to her, whom she was unable to summon up fully to remembrance. Her fears evaporated, she forgot that it was Cardillac's murderer kneeling before her, she spoke in the pleasant tones of calm benevolence characteristic of her, and said, 'Now, Brusson, what do you have to tell me?' He, still on his knees, heaved a sigh of deep, ardent melancholy and then replied, 'Oh my honoured, most esteemed lady, has every trace of remembrance of me thus fled?' Mlle de Scudéri, studying him more attentively, replied that she did indeed detect in his features a resemblance to some person dear to her, and that it was this resemblance alone that he had to thank for the fact she could overcome the deep revulsion she felt at the presence of a murderer, and calmly give him a hearing. Brusson, deeply wounded by these words, rose quickly to his feet and, his eyes fixed darkly on the ground, took a step backwards. Then he said, in a hollow voice, 'So have you quite forgotten Anne Guiot? It is her son Olivier, the boy that you often used to dandle on your knees, who is standing before you.'

'Ah, for the love of all the saints!' cried Mlle de Scudéri, burying her face in her hands and sinking back into her cushions. She had cause enough to react with such dismay. Anne Guiot, the daughter of an impoverished burgher, had from her earliest childhood lived in the home of Mlle de Scudéri, who had brought her up with the greatest care and devotion, as a mother brings up her own dear child. When she had grown to adulthood, a handsome, honest young man named Claude Brusson had come along and courted the girl. As he was an exceptionally skilled watchmaker, bound to earn a decent living in Paris, and as Anne had fallen deeply in love with him, Mlle de Scudéri had absolutely no hesitation in agreeing to the marriage of her foster-daughter. The young couple moved into their own home together, lived in tranquil domestic happiness, and their bond of love was made even stronger by the birth of a wonderful bonny boy, the very image of his fair mother.

Mlle de Scudéri idolised little Olivier, whom she took off his mother's hands for hours and days at a time, hugging and cuddling him. So it came about that the boy grew perfectly used to her, and was as happy to spend time with her as with his own mother. Three years went by, and the growing envy of Brusson's fellow artisans at his success finally resulted in depriving him of any work, so that in the end he could barely earn enough to feed himself. Whereupon he felt a yearning for the beautiful city of Geneva where he came from, with the result that his little family moved there, despite the resistance of Mlle de Scudéri, who promised to support them to the very best of her abilities. Anne wrote just once or twice to her foster-mother, and then fell silent, so that Mlle de Scudéri could only deduce that their happy life in Brusson's homeland did not allow any memory of their earlier days to surface.

'Oh how dreadful,' exclaimed Mlle de Scudéri, as soon as she had begun to recover from the shock. 'Oh how dreadful! You are Olivier? The son of my Anne! – And now!'

'To be sure,' retorted Olivier with calm self-composure, 'to be sure, honoured lady, you would never have guessed that the boy that you used to cuddle like the most affectionate mother, dandling him on your lap and pushing sweet after sweet into his mouth, and calling him by the most darling names, would one day, as a grown lad, stand before you accused of a dreadful murder! I am not above all reproach; the *Chambre ardente* can with justice accuse me of a crime; but, as I hope to die in a state of grace, even if it be at the executioner's hand, I am innocent of any murder, and it was not through me or any fault of mine that the unhappy Cardillac met his death!' – At these words, Olivier started to tremble and totter on his feet. Mlle de Scudéri silently motioned him to a small armchair next to where he was standing. He slowly sank into it.

'I have had time enough,' he began, 'to prepare myself for this interview with you that I consider as the last favour granted me by reconciled Heaven, and to work up as much calm and composure as are necessary for me to recount to you the story of my dreadful and unprecedented misfortune. Show enough compassion as to hear me out calmly, however much you may be surprised and indeed horrified to discover a secret that you could never have guessed at. If only my poor father had never left Paris!... So far as I can remember Geneva, I can still see myself drenched in my disconsolate parents' tears, and brought to tears myself by their laments, even though I could not understand their cause. Later I gained a clear sense, a full awareness, of the oppressive neediness and wretchedness in which my parents lived. My father was disappointed in all his hopes. Bent down by deep sorrow, quite overwhelmed, he died at the very moment he had succeeded in finding me a position as an apprentice to a goldsmith. My mother spoke a great deal of you, she wanted to pour out her laments to you, but then the despondency produced by misery overcame her. That, and also the false sense of shame that often nags at a mortally wounded heart, held her back from fulfilling her wish. A few months after my father's death, my mother followed him to the grave.'

'Poor Anne! Poor Anne!' exclaimed Mlle de Scudéri, over-powered by grief. 'Thanks and praise be to the eternal powers of Heaven, that she has passed on, and so cannot see her beloved son in the executioner's hand, branded by the mark of infamy.' At this, Olivier cried aloud, darting wild and terrible eyes upwards. There was a disturbance outside, and the noise of people moving about. 'Ha ha!' said Olivier with a bitter smile. 'Desgrais is waking up his cronies, as if I could escape from *here*! But I must continue! – I was harshly treated by my master, despite soon being the best at my work and indeed eventually far surpassing him. It so happened that one day a stranger came into our workshop to buy some jewellery. But the minute he saw a fine necklace that I'd made, he gave me a friendly pat on the shoulders and, still eyeing the piece, said, "Well, well! my young friend, that is really excellent work. Truth to tell, I can't think who could do any better than you, if not René Cardillac, who admittedly is the best goldsmith in the world. You ought to go and work for him; he will be very happy to take you into his workshop, for only *you* can assist him in his artistic work, and from him alone can you still learn something in return." The stranger's words had made a deep impression on my soul. From then on I felt restless in Geneva, and was strongly tempted to leave. I finally managed to free myself from my master. I came to Paris. René Cardillac received me coldly and curtly. I refused to give up, and told him he must give me work, even of the most insignificant kind. I was given the task of making a small ring. When I brought the work to him, he stared at me with his gleaming eyes, as if he wanted to peer into my innermost soul. Then he said, "You are a competent, upright apprentice, you can come and work for me and help me out in my workshop. I'll pay you well, you will be satisfied with me." Cardillac kept his word. I had been with him for several weeks before I saw Madelon, who, if I am not mistaken, was staying with an aunt of Cardillac's in the country at the time. Finally she returned. Oh you eternal power of Heaven, what did I feel when I saw that angel! Has anyone ever loved as much as I did! And now! – Oh Madelon!'

Olivier was too disconsolate to speak. He buried his head in his hands and shook with sobs. Finally, forcing himself to fight down the wild grief that had gripped him, he continued his story.

'Madelon looked at me with friendly eyes. She came more and more often into the workshop. I was thrilled to realise she loved me. However strictly Cardillac watched us, many a surreptitious handclasp acted as a sign of the troth we were plighting, and Cardillac seemed not to notice a thing. I planned, once I had earned his goodwill, and managed to become a master in my own right, to ask for Madelon's hand. One morning, as I was just about to begin my work, Cardillac came and stood before me, anger and contempt in his sombre eyes. "I don't need your work any more," he began, "I want you out of my house this very hour, and don't let me ever set eyes on you again. I don't have to tell you why I won't stand your presence here any longer. You poor devil, the sweet fruit you craved for hangs too high for your grasp!" I wanted to talk to him, but he seized me in his strong grip and threw me out at the door, so violently that I fell headlong and was badly wounded on my head and arm. Filled with indignation and racked by sorrow, I left the house, and finally found a good-natured acquaintance of mine living on the outskirts of the *faubourg* St-Martin, who put me up in his attic. I had no peace, no rest. At night-time I prowled round Cardillac's house, imagining that Madelon would hear my sighs and laments, and perhaps manage to speak to me unobserved from her window. All sorts of daring plans kept going round in my head, and I hoped I could persuade her to carry them out. Next to Cardillac's house in the rue St-Nicaise there is a high wall with niches and old, half-crumbling statues. One night I stood close to one of these statues, and gazed up at the windows of the house overlooking the courtyard that the wall encloses. Then I suddenly spotted a light in Cardillac's workshop. It was midnight; never before had Cardillac been awake at that time, he was in the habit of retiring to his bed on the stroke of nine. My heart was hammering with anxious premonitions; I tried to think of some way of gaining an entry. But the light immediately disappeared. I pressed myself up against the statue and into the niche, but then I leapt back in horror, feeling a reciprocal pressure, as if the statue had come to life. In the grey glimmer of the night, I saw the stone slowly turn, and from behind it a dark figure slipped out and padded off down the street. I sprang back towards the statue, but it was standing right up against the wall as before. Involuntarily, as if driven by some inner force, I slipped after the figure in the street. Right in front of an image of the Virgin Mary, the figure glanced round, and the full gleam of the bright lamp burning before the image fell onto his face. It was Cardillac! An inconceivable anxiety, an uncanny dread overwhelmed me. As if under some magic spell I had no choice but to go on – following the ghostly sleepwalker. For that is what I thought the master was, despite the fact that it was not a full moon, which is when such spooks tend to disturb our sleep. Finally Cardillac stepped sideways and disappeared into the deep shadows. By the brief but recognisable noise he made as he cleared his throat, I realised that he had stepped into the entrance of a house. What did it mean; what was he up to? – That was what I wondered in my astonishment, and pressed myself close up to the houses. Shortly afterwards, a man came along singing and tra-la-laing with a bright plume on his hat and clinking spurs at his feet. Like a tiger pouncing on its prey, Cardillac leapt out of his lair and threw himself at the man, who instantly fell to the ground with a death-rattle. With a cry of horror I jumped out: Cardillac was bending over the man on the ground. "Master Cardillac, what are you doing?" I shouted. "Damn you!" bellowed Cardillac, darted quick as lightning past me, and vanished. Quite beside myself, barely able to take a step, I went up to the man he had attacked. I knelt down at his side, thinking that perhaps he could still be saved, but there was not a breath of life still in him. In my mortal anguish I was barely aware of the fact that I had been surrounded by police. "Another man laid low by those devils!" – "Hey there!" – "Young man, what are you doing there?" – "Are you one of the gang?" – "Up you get!", they all shouted together as they laid hands on me. I was barely able to stammer that I couldn't possibly have committed such a foul crime, and begged them to let me go. Then one of them held up a lantern to my face and exclaimed with a laugh: "Why, it's Olivier Brusson, the goldsmith's apprentice, who works for our honest, upstanding Master René Cardillac! Oh yes, *he*'s the one going round murdering people in the streets! Looks just the type to me – it's typical of murderers to stand weeping and wailing by the body and let themselves get caught… What happened, young man? – Out with it!"

'"Right in front of me," I said, "a man jumped out at this one, struck him down and ran away as fast as lightning, while I started to cry for help. But I wanted to see if the victim could still be saved."

'"No, son," exclaimed one of the men who had lifted up the corpse. "He's dead and gone; as usual the dagger has gone right through the heart."

'"Damnation," said another, "we arrived too late, just like the day before yesterday"; whereupon they went off with the corpse.

'Words cannot express how I felt; I pinched myself to see if I were in the grip of some bad dream, and I imagined I would soon wake up and marvel at this crazy delusion. Cardillac – the father of my Madelon, a foul murderer! – I had slumped onto the stone steps of a house. Day was gradually starting to break, an officer's hat, richly adorned with plumes, lay on the cobbles in front of me. Cardillac's bloody crime, committed on that same spot where I was sitting, appeared to me in all its ghastliness. Filled with horror, I ran off.

'Quite bewildered and almost unable to gather my thoughts, I was sitting in my garret when the door opened and René Cardillac stepped in. "For Christ's sake! What do you want?" I shouted at him. He, paying not the slightest heed, came up to me and smiled at me with a tranquillity and affability that only increased my inner revulsion. He pulled up an old, rickety stool and sat in front of me: I was unable to lift my body from the straw bed onto which I had flung myself. "Now Olivier," he began, "how are you, you poor boy? I behaved much too hastily when I threw you so horribly out of my house; I miss you every minute, the place is empty without you. Right now I'm planning a piece of work that I can't bring off without your help. How would you like to come and work for me again? – No answer? – Yes, I know I have offended you. I didn't want to make any bones about the fact that it was because I knew you were flirting with my Madelon. But then I thought it all through a bit more carefully, and decided that given your skill, your capacity for hard work, and your loyalty, I could wish for no better son-in-law than you. So come along with me and find out how you can win Madelon to be your bride."

'Cardillac's words cut me to the heart, I trembled at his wickedness, and couldn't utter a single word. "You're hesitating?" he continued sharply, as his gleaming eyes bored through me. "You're hesitating? – Perhaps you can't come with me today, you have other plans? – Perhaps you want to call on Desgrais, or even present yourself to d'Argenson or La Reynie. Take care, my lad, that the claws you want to see seizing on others don't sink into you instead and tear you apart." At that point my outraged feelings suddenly found expression. "May those," I cried, "may those with gruesome crimes on their consciences fear those names you just mentioned; I don't – I have nothing to do with them."

'"Actually," resumed Cardillac, "actually, Olivier, it will do you honour if you work for me, for me, the most famous master of our age, universally held in the greatest esteem for his loyalty and uprightness, so much so that any malicious slander would rebound heavily on the slanderer's own head. – As far as Madelon is concerned, I have to confess to you that you owe my pliability to her alone. She loves you with an ardour that I can hardly credit in such a tender child. The minute you had gone, she fell to my feet, threw her arms round my knees and confessed as the tears poured down her face that she couldn't live without you. I thought she was simply imagining, as young things in love so often do, that she wanted to die just because the first baby-faced lad to come along had smiled at her. But indeed, my Madelon really did turn weak and sickly, and when I wanted to talk her out of the whole crazy business, she called your name a hundred times over. What could I do, at the end of the day? I didn't want her to succumb to despair. Yesterday evening I told her I would give my blessing to it all and come and fetch you today. And overnight she blossomed like a rose and is waiting for you now, quite beside herself with her amorous yearnings." – May the eternal power of Heaven forgive me, but I myself don't know how it came about that I was suddenly standing in Cardillac's house, and Madelon was crying out in joy: "Olivier – my Olivier – my beloved – my husband"; she rushed up to me, flung her arms round me, and pressed me close to her breast, so that overpowered by the most intense ecstasy I swore by the Blessed Virgin and all the saints never to leave her!'

Shaken by the memory of this decisive moment, Olivier had

to pause. Mlle de Scudéri, filled with horror at the crime of a man she had considered the epitome of virtue and probity, exclaimed: 'How dreadful! – René Cardillac, a member of that gang of murderers that for so long has made of our good city a den of thieves?'

'What are you saying, my lady?' said Olivier. 'A member of *what* gang? There never was such a gang. It was Cardillac *alone* who with terrible energy sought out and found his victims throughout the whole city. It was the very fact that he worked *alone* that meant that he could carry out his crimes with impunity, and that made it difficult, no, impossible, to find any trace of the murderer. – But allow me to continue, the rest of the story will reveal to you the secrets of the most despicable and at the same time most unhappy of all men.

'The situation in which I now found myself at my master's can easily be imagined. The die was cast, I couldn't step back. At times I had the impression that I myself had been Cardillac's accomplice in murder; only in Madelon's love did I forget the inner pain tormenting me, only with her did I succeed in eradicating every outward trace of my nameless distress. When I worked with the old man in the workshop, I couldn't look him in the face. I could barely utter a word, such was the shudder of horror that ran through me on finding myself next to such a dreadful character, who performed to the full all the virtues of a faithful, affectionate father and a good burgher, while night veiled his crimes. Madelon, the pious child, as pure as an angel, idolised him with her devoted love. My heart was pierced whenever I thought that if the villain were ever unmasked and struck down by vengeance, she, a victim of all of Satan's hellish cunning, would be bound to succumb to the cruellest despair. This was enough for me to stay silent, even if I had to suffer a criminal's death for it.

Although I had gathered a fair bit from the words of the police, Cardillac's crimes, their motivation, and the way he carried them out, remained a puzzle to me: but I didn't have to wait long for it to be cleared up. One day Cardillac, who at other times, much to my disgust, always performed his work joking and laughing in the greatest good humour, seemed grave and lost in his thoughts. Suddenly he threw down the piece of jewellery he was just then working on, so that the gems and pearls rolled away, stood up vehemently and said: "Olivier! Things can't go on between us like this any longer, I can't stand this relationship. What the craftiest guile of Desgrais and his cronies was unable to discover, chance played into your hands and allowed you to find out. You have observed me in my nocturnal labours, that my evil star drives me to, so powerfully I cannot resist it. And it was *your* evil star that let you follow me, hiding you in an impenetrable veil, and making your footsteps so light you could move about as inaudibly as the smallest creature, so that I, who in the deepest, darkest night can see as clearly as a tiger, and can hear the faintest sound, the mere buzz of a fly, from streets away – I didn't notice you. Your evil star has brought you, my partner, to me. Given your situation here, there can be no thought of your betraying me. So you may as well know everything."

'"No more will I be your partner, you hypocritical villain." – This is what I wanted to cry, but the inner horror that seized me at Cardillac's words choked my voice. Instead of words I could only utter an incomprehensible noise. Cardillac sat back in his armchair. He wiped the sweat from his forehead. Appearing hard-pressed by the memory of former times, he seemed to pull himself together with an effort. Finally he began, "Wise men have a great deal to say about the strange impressions that expectant women sometimes undergo, and of

60

the remarkable influence that a vivid, involuntary impression may exert from without on the child. I was told an amazing story about my mother. As she was out and about in her first month of pregnancy with me, she found herself with some other women watching a brilliant court festivity that was being given in the Trianon.[9] Her gaze happened to fall on a cavalier wearing Spanish clothes and a dazzling jewelled chain around his neck which she simply couldn't take her eyes off. Every fibre of her being was filled with desire for the gleaming gemstones that seemed to her a more than earthly treasure. The same cavalier had many years previously, when my mother was not yet married, made an attempt on her virtue, but had been sent packing with expressions of revulsion. My mother recognised him again, but this time it was as if in the radiance of the gleaming diamonds he were a being of a higher kind, the epitome of everything most handsome. The cavalier noticed my mother's yearning, ardent glances. He thought that now he would meet with better luck than before. He managed to get close to her, and even to lure her away from her acquaintances to a lonely spot. There he clasped her in an impassioned embrace; my mother started reaching out for the beautiful chain, but at that same moment he sank down and dragged my mother with him to the ground. Whether because he suffered a sudden stroke, or for some other reason – there he lay, dead. My mother's efforts to struggle free of the corpse's arms, now rigid in death, were in vain. With his hollow eyes, their sight extinguished, still gazing at her, the dead man rolled with her on the ground. Her shrill cries for help finally came to the ears of some people passing by in the distance, who came hurrying up and released her from the arms of her gruesome lover. The horror of it all forced my mother to take to her bed, gravely ill. Both she and I were given up for lost, but she recovered, and her delivery was more successful than anyone could have anticipated.

'"But the alarm she had felt at that dreadful moment had affected *me*. My evil star had risen and darted its rays down on me, setting alight in me one of the strangest and most pernicious of passions. Already in earliest childhood I was more fond of sparkling diamonds and golden jewellery than of anything else. This was considered to be a perfectly ordinary childish inclination. But it looked like something else entirely when, as a boy, I began to steal gold and jewels wherever I could get my hands on them. Like the most experienced connoisseur I could instinctively distinguish between fake and authentic jewellery. Only the latter attracted me; I left adulterated and minted gold untouched. This inborn desire was forced to give way under my father's cruel punishments. Simply so I could get close to gold and precious stones, I turned to the profession of goldsmith. I worked passionately and soon became the best master in this art. Now began a period in which the inborn drive, repressed for so long, forced its way violently up and grew in power, undermining all around it. The minute I had completed and delivered a piece of jewellery, I fell into a state of inconsolable unrest that robbed me of sleep, health and the very courage to face life. – Like a phantom, the person for whom I had produced my work stood day and night in front of my eyes, decked out with my jewellery, and a voice whispered in my ears: 'But it's yours – it's yours – so take it! – what use are diamonds to the dead?' Finally I resorted to robber's tricks. I had access to the houses of the great, I quickly seized every opportunity, no lock could withstand my skill and before long the jewellery that I had produced was back in my hands. But soon even this did not drive away my restlessness. That uncanny voice still sounded in my ears, mocking me and calling: 'Ho ho! Your jewels are being worn by a dead man!' I myself did not know how it came about that I felt such an unspeakable hatred towards those for whom I produced jewellery. Yes! Deep within me a murderous lust for blood stirred against them, so strong that I myself trembled at it.

'"At that time I bought this house. I had concluded the sale with the owner; here in this room we were sitting together pleased at the business we had just wrapped up, drinking a bottle of wine. Night had fallen, I wanted to leave, and my vendor said: 'Listen, Master René, before you go, I must acquaint you with a secret of this house.' Thereupon he opened that cupboard set into the wall, pushed back the far wall, stepped into a small chamber, bent down, and lifted up a trapdoor. We went down some steep, narrow steps, came to a narrow little door, which he opened, and stepped out into the open courtyard. Now the old man, my vendor, walked up to the wall, pushed a barely protruding iron knob, and immediately part of the wall swung open so that a man could comfortably slip through the opening and reach the street. You ought to see this little invention sometime, Olivier: it was probably devised by sly monks from the monastery that once stood here, so they could slip in and out on the quiet. It's a piece of wood, stuccoed and whitewashed just on the outside, into which a statue has been fitted from the outside, also really in wood but looking just like stone: the whole thing is able to turn on hidden hinges. – Dark thoughts rose within me when I saw this arrangement; it seemed to me as if such deeds were in the offing as still remained hidden from me. I had just delivered to a gentleman at Court a rich piece of jewellery, which, as I knew full well was meant for a dancing girl of the opera. My mortal torment soon overcame me – the phantom dogged my steps – the lisping Satan whispered in my ear! – I moved into the house. Sweating blood in my anguish, I tossed and turned sleeplessly on my bed! In my mind's eye I could see the man slipping off to his dancer with my piece of jewellery. Filled with rage I leapt up, threw my coat round me, went down the secret steps, out through the wall into the rue St-Nicaise. Along he came, I fell on him, he cried out, but holding him tight from behind I plunged my dagger into his heart – the jewellery was mine! – Once the deed was done, I felt such a sense of peace and satisfaction in my heart as I had never felt before. The phantom had vanished, and Satan's voice had fallen silent. Now I knew what my evil star required, and I must yield to it or drown!

'"Now you can understand all my deeds and actions, Olivier! Don't think that, because I have to do what I cannot help but do, I have completely abandoned those feelings of sympathy and pity that are supposed to be implanted in man's nature. You know how difficult I find it to deliver a piece of jewellery; how I flatly refuse to work for many people whose deaths I do not wish, that indeed, knowing as I do that on the next morning bloodshed will drive away my phantom, I content myself on certain days with a well-delivered punch which lays out the possessor of my jewellery and delivers it into my hands."

'Having said all this, Cardillac led me into the secret vault and allowed me to look at his jewel cabinet. The King himself does not possess anything more valuable. On each piece of jewellery hung a precise indication written on a small label, saying for whom it had been made, and when it had been taken back, through burglary, robbery, or murder. "On your wedding day," said Cardillac in a hollow, solemn voice, "on your wedding day, Olivier, you will swear to me, your hand on the image of the crucified Christ, a sacred oath that as soon as I am dead you will reduce all these riches to dust, by a means that I will disclose to you. I do not want any human being, least of all Madelon and you, to come into possession of a hoard that has been purchased with blood." Caught in this labyrinth of crime, torn between love and revulsion, rapture and horror, I was like the damned soul whom a fair angel is beckoning upwards with a gentle smile, while Satan holds him tight in his burning claws, so that the pious angel's loving smile, in which is reflected all the bliss of the highest heaven, turns into the grimmest of all his torments. – I thought of flight – even of suicide – but Madelon! – Blame me, blame me, my honoured lady, for being too weak to take drastic measures to fight down a passion which kept me enchained to crime: but am I not atoning for it with a shameful death?

'One day Cardillac came home in an unusually cheerful frame of mind. He hugged Madelon, glanced at me in the friendliest way, drank a bottle of fine wine at table, as he usually did only on high days and holidays, and sang and rejoiced. Madelon had left us, I wanted to get back to the workshop: "Stay where you are, my boy," exclaimed Cardillac, "no more work today, let's drink another toast to the health of the worthiest, most excellent lady in Paris!" Once I had clinked glasses with him and he had drained a full glass, he said, "Tell me, Olivier! how do you like these verses:

"'Un amant qui craint les voleurs
n'est point digne d'amour!"

'He went on to recount what had happened in the rooms of Mme de Maintenon with you and the King, and added that he had always honoured you like no other human being, and that

65

you, graced with such high virtue, before which the evil star was rendered pallid and powerless, could never, even when wearing the finest jewels of his making, arouse any evil phantom, or any thoughts of murder. "Listen Olivier," he said, "to what I have decided. A long time ago I was commissioned to make a necklace and bracelets for Henrietta of England, and deliver the gems for it myself. The work succeeded like no other, but it tore my heart to think that I would have to give up the piece of jewellery that had become the pride and joy among all my treasures. You know how the unfortunate princess was treacherously assassinated. I got my jewellery back, and now I want to send it to Mlle de Scudéri as a sign of my respect and my gratitude. Apart from the fact that Mlle de Scudéri thus receives an eloquent token of her triumph, I thereby also pour scorn on Desgrais and his sidekicks, as they deserve. You must take the jewellery to her."

'The moment Cardillac uttered your name, my lady, it was as if a black veil had been torn away, and the lovely, luminous image of my happy early childhood rose again in all its vivid, gleaming colours. A wonderful sense of consolation filled my soul, a ray of hope before which the dark spirits vanished. Cardillac was able to perceive the impression his words had made on me and to interpret them in his own way. "My plan," he said, "seems to meet with your favour. I am happy to admit that a voice from deep within, quite different from the one which demands blood sacrifice like some voracious predator, commanded me to do this. – I often feel really strange – an inner anguish, a fear of something dreadful, the horror of which floats towards me from some distant beyond into this time-bound world, and seizes me forcibly. Then it even seems to me that what my evil star has started to work through me might be blamed on my immortal soul, even though the latter had no part in it. In this frame of mind I decided to make a beautiful diamond crown for the Blessed Virgin in the church of St Eustache. But that incomprehensible anguish overcame me all the more strongly each time I tried to begin the work, so I completely abandoned it. Now it occurs to me that I myself can humbly offer a sacrifice to virtue and piety, and entreat effective mediation, by sending to Mlle de Scudéri the finest piece of jewellery that I have ever made."

'Cardillac, acquainted in the greatest detail with your whole way of life, my lady, gave me the ways and means as well as the hour, telling me how and when I should deliver the jewellery that he enclosed in a trim casket. My whole being was filled with rapture, for heaven itself was showing me, through the wicked Cardillac, how I could escape from the hell in which, a rejected sinner, I was languishing. So I thought. Completely against Cardillac's will I wanted to contact you. As Anne Brusson's son, and as your foster-child, I wanted to throw myself at your feet and explain everything to you, everything. Moved by the unspeakable misery threatening poor, innocent Madelon if the facts came to light, you would keep the secret; but your noble and astute mind would surely find a more certain way of putting a stop to the despicable wickedness of Cardillac without betraying our secret. Don't ask me *which* way, I don't know – but that you would save Madelon and myself I was firmly convinced in my soul, just as I believe in the consoling succour of the Blessed Virgin.

'You know, my lady, that my intention that night went amiss. I didn't lose all hope of succeeding on another occasion. Then it so happened that Cardillac lost all his cheerfulness. He wandered desperately around, staring in front of him, murmuring incomprehensible words, and lashing out with his hands as if fighting off some enemy; and his mind seemed tormented by evil thoughts. He had been behaving like this for a whole morning. Finally he sat down at his work table, jumped up again ill-humouredly, looked through the window, and said in grave and lugubrious tones, "I wish Henrietta of England had worn my jewels!"

'The words filled me with horror. Now I knew that his demented mind was once more in thrall to the dreadful phantom of death, and that Satan's voice had spoken loud and clear in his ears. I saw your life threatened by foul and devilish murder. If Cardillac could only get his jewellery back, your life would be saved. With every instant the danger increased. So it was that I met you on the Pont Neuf, forced my way through to your carriage, and threw you that note imploring you to hand the jewellery you had been given back to Cardillac. You did not come. My anxiety increased and turned into despair when, on the next day, Cardillac could talk of nothing other than the precious jewellery that had appeared before his eyes that night. I could only interpret this to mean *your* jewellery, and I was certain that he was brooding over some murderous plan that he had certainly decided to carry out that night. I had to rescue you, even at the cost of Cardillac's life.

'As soon as Cardillac had locked himself in as usual after his evening prayer, I climbed out of a window into the courtyard, slipped though the opening in the wall, and took up my position not far away, hidden in deep shadow. I didn't have to wait long before Cardillac emerged and slipped off quietly down the street. I went after him. We headed down the rue St-Honoré, my heart racing. Cardillac had suddenly disappeared. I decided to position myself by your front door. Then along came singing and tra-la-laing past me, just as before, on the occasion when chance had made of me a spectator of Cardillac's murderous crime, an officer who went by without noticing me.

'But that very minute a black figure leapt out and attacked him. It was Cardillac. This death I could prevent; with a loud cry I reached the spot in two or three strides – but it was not the officer who fell to the ground mortally wounded and uttering a death rattle. The officer dropped the dagger, drew his rapier from its sheath, and stood ready to fight, thinking I was the murderer's accomplice; but then he quickly hurried away when he saw that, paying no attention to him, I was intent on examining the corpse. Cardillac was still alive. I heaved him up onto my shoulders, having first hidden on my person the dagger that the officer had dropped, and dragged him with difficulty back home, through the secret passage and up into the workshop.

'The rest you know. You can see, my honoured lady, that my only crime consists in not having betrayed Madelon's father to the courts and thereby putting a stop to his crimes. I am innocent of any murder. – No torture will wring the secret of Cardillac's crimes from me. I do not want to go against the eternal power which concealed the father's gruesome murders from his virtuous daughter, or let all the wretchedness of the past and of her whole existence break in on her even now, for it would kill her; nor do I want the world's vengeance to dig up Cardillac's corpse from the earth that covers him, and allow the executioner to brand his mouldering bones with the mark of infamy. – No! – My soul's beloved will weep for me as an innocent victim, and time will alleviate her pain; but she would never get over the distress of learning of her father's hellish deeds!'

Olivier fell silent, but then a flood of tears suddenly burst from his eyes, he flung himself at the feet of Mlle de Scudéri and implored her, 'You are convinced of my innocence – of course you are! Have mercy on me, tell me, how are things with Madelon?' Mlle de Scudéri called Martinière, and a few moments later Madelon rushed in and threw her arms round Olivier's neck. 'Now you're here, everything is all right – I just knew that noblest of ladies would save you!' So Madelon kept exclaiming, and Olivier forgot his fate and the danger he was still in; he felt free, and blissfully happy. In the most moving tones they both lamented all that they had suffered, and embraced each other again and wept for rapture at having found each other again.

Even if Mlle de Scudéri had not already been convinced of Olivier's innocence, she would have believed in it now as she saw the two of them, in the bliss of their most tender bond of love forgetting the world and their wretchedness and their unspeakable suffering. 'No,' she cried, 'only a pure heart is capable of such blessed oblivion.'

The bright beams of morning shone through the windows. Desgrais knocked gently on the door of the room and re-minded them it was time for Olivier to be taken away, since to postpone it any longer would attract attention. The lovers had to part.

The dark premonitions in which Mlle de Scudéri's heart had been enveloped since Brusson's first entry into her house had now been given living and fearful shape. She saw the son of her beloved Anna innocently embroiled in a situation such that it seemed almost impossible to rescue him from a shameful death. She honoured the youth's heroic intention to die burdened with guilt rather than betray a secret that must cause the death of his Madelon. In the entire realm of possibility she could find no means of wresting this most unhappy man from the cruel tribunal. And yet she was firmly convinced in her soul that she must shrink from no sacrifice to avert the injustice that cried aloud to heaven and that was about to be committed. She wrestled with all kinds of projects and plans, verging on the thoroughly hazardous, and then rejected them no sooner than she had conceived them. Every gleam of hope faded away, so that she was on the point of despair. But Madelon's unconditional, pious and childlike trust, and the transfiguration with which she spoke of her beloved, who now, she thought, exonerated of all guilt, would soon be embracing her as his wife, gave her new courage, so greatly and deeply was she moved by it.

So as finally to do something concrete, Mlle de Scudéri wrote a long letter to La Reynie, telling him that Olivier Brusson had demonstrated his complete and indubitable innocence of Cardillac's death to her, and that only his heroic decision to take with him to the grave a secret that would, if revealed, bring ruin to Innocence and Virtue themselves was holding him back from making a confession to the court that would inevitably free him from the dreadful suspicion that he was Cardillac's murderer or that he belonged to the gang of vile murderers. Mlle de Scudéri had summoned up everything that fervent zeal and intellectual eloquence could do to soften the hard heart of La Reynie. A few hours later, La Reynie replied that he was heartily pleased to learn that Olivier Brusson had completely justified himself in the eyes of his noble, worthy protectress. As for Olivier's heroic decision to take with him to the grave a secret also relevant to the case, he was sorry that the *Chambre ardente* was unable to honour such heroism, but must seek through the most potent means available to break it. He hoped within three days to be in possession of this strange secret that would probably shed light on many of the amazing things that had occurred.

Mlle de Scudéri knew only too well what the terrible La Reynie meant when he alluded to those means that were to break Brusson's heroism. Now it was certain that the threat of torture was hanging over the unhappy young man. In her mortal anguish, Mlle de Scudéri finally had the idea that, merely to obtain a postponement, the advice of someone versed in the law could be useful. Pierre Arnaud d'Andilly was at that time the most famous lawyer in Paris. His profound knowledge and wide-ranging understanding were matched by his probity and virtue. Mlle de Scudéri went to see him and told him everything, insofar as this was possible without giving away Brusson's secret. She thought that d'Andilly would be all too glad to take on the case of the innocent man, but her hope was most bitterly disappointed. D'Andilly had listened calmly to everything and then replied smilingly with Boileau's words: '*Le vrai peut quelque fois n'être pas vraisemblable*.'[10] – He proved to Mlle de Scudéri that the most eloquent grounds for suspicion all spoke against Brusson, that La Reynie's behaviour could in no way be called cruel or over-hasty, but was, in fact, perfectly legal, and that he could not have behaved in any other way without violating the duties of a judge. He, d'Andilly, would not trust himself to be able, even if he put up the most skilful defence, to save Brusson from torture. Only Brusson himself could do that, either by making an honest confession or at least by recounting in the most exact detail the circumstances surrounding the murder of Cardillac, that would then perhaps give an opportunity for further investigations. 'In that case, I will throw myself at the King's feet and implore him for mercy,' said Mlle de Scudéri, quite beside herself, her voice half choked by tears. 'Don't do that,' cried d'Andilly, 'don't for heaven's sake do that, my lady! – Keep that as a last resort, for once it has failed, you have lost your chance once and for all. The King will never pardon a criminal of *that* kind: the bitterest reproaches of his people, who feel so much in danger, would fall on him. It is possible that Brusson will, by disclosing his secret or else through some other means, find a way of lifting the suspicion levelled against him. Then it will be time to implore the King for mercy, when he will not ask what has been proven or not proven in a court of law, but will take counsel of his own inner convictions.' Mlle de Scudéri was reluctantly forced to agree, bowing to the wide experience of d'Andilly. Sunk in deep distress, thinking and thinking what, by the Blessed Virgin and all the saints, she could do now to rescue the unhappy Brusson, she was sitting late at evening in her room, when Martinière stepped in and announced the Count de Miossens, colonel of the King's Guard, who urgently desired to speak to her mistress.

'Forgive me,' said Miossens, bowing with all the good manners of a soldier, 'forgive me, my lady, for disturbing you so late at night and at such an inconvenient hour. We soldiers cannot choose our moment, and in any case I have only a couple of words to say. It is Olivier Brusson who brings me to you.' Mlle de Scudéri, in the greatest suspense as to what she was now going to hear, exclaimed aloud, 'Olivier Brusson? that most unfortunate of men? – What have you got to do with him?'

'I guessed,' continued Miossens with a smile, 'that your protégé's name would suffice for you to lend a favourable ear to what I have to say. The whole world is convinced of Brusson's guilt. I know that you harbour a different opinion, one that admittedly seems to rest only on the assertions of the accused, as everyone has said. It's different in my case. Nobody can be more convinced than I that Brusson is innocent of Cardillac's murder.'

'Tell me, oh tell me,' cried Mlle de Scudéri, her eyes

gleaming with rapture. 'It was I,' said Miossens emphatically, 'it was I who struck down the old goldsmith in the rue St-Honoré not far from your house.'

'By all the saints – you! – you!' cried Mlle de Scudéri.

'And,' continued Miossens, 'and I can swear to you, my lady, that I am proud of my deed. You should know that Cardillac was the foulest, most hypocritical villain, that it was he who went round treacherously murdering and robbing, and managed to evade every trap for so long. I myself don't know how it was that an inner suspicion arose in me against the old villain when, full of evident disquiet, he brought me the jewellery I had ordered, and asked for the details of the person for whom I intended it, and then in the most cunning fashion cross-questioned my valet as to when I habitually went to visit a certain lady. – I had long ago noticed that the unfortunate victims of those most abominable robberies all bore the same fatal wound. I was sure that the murderer had mastered his blow, one that had to kill its victim straight away, and that he reckoned on its always being effective. If it failed, it meant a struggle on equal terms. This led me to employ a pre-cautionary measure so simple I can't understand why others did not come up with it long ago and thereby save themselves from the murderer's menace. I wore a light breastplate under my jacket. Cardillac fell on me from behind. He threw his arms round me with the strength of a giant, but his blow, aimed with great precision, glanced off the iron. At the same instant I escaped from his clutches, and stabbed him in the breast with the dagger I was holding ready.'

'And you were silent,' asked Mlle de Scudéri, 'you didn't go to tell the courts what had happened?'

'Allow me,' continued Miossens, 'allow me, my lady, to point out that such a deposition might have involved me, if not in my own ruin, at least in the most terrible trial. Would La Reynie, sniffing out crime everywhere, have believed me if I had accused the honest Cardillac, the model of all piety and virtue, of being the wanted murderer? What if the sword of justice had turned its point against me myself?'

'That was impossible,' cried Mlle de Scudéri, 'your noble birth – your rank…'

'Oh,' continued Miossens, 'just remember the Marshall de Luxembourg, who merely by getting Le Sage to read his horoscope came under suspicion of causing death by poisoning and was locked in the Bastille. No, by St Denis, I am not going to surrender an hour's freedom, nor even the tip of my ear, to that madman La Reynie who is so keen to set his knife at all our throats.'

'But in this way you will bring the innocent Brusson to the scaffold?' interrupted Mlle de Scudéri.

'Innocent?' retorted Miossens. 'Innocent, my lady – is that what you call the heinous Cardillac's accomplice? – the one who was at his side in his misdeeds? The one who has deserved death a thousand times over? – No, in truth, *he* will die with justice, and the reason I have disclosed the complete chain of events to you, my most honoured lady, was that I presumed you would be able to use my secret in some way for the benefit of your protégé, but without delivering me into the hands of the *Chambre ardente.*'

Mlle de Scudéri, inwardly enraptured to see her conviction of Brusson's innocence confirmed so decisively, did not hesitate to disclose everything to the Count, who already knew of Cardillac's crime, and to request him to go with her to see d'Andilly. He would be told everything, under the seal of confidentiality, and he would then give them advice as to what to do next.

D'Andilly, once Mlle de Scudéri had recounted everything to him in the most precise detail, asked once more about apparently trivial particularities. He especially asked Count Miossens whether he too was firmly convinced that he had been attacked by Cardillac, and whether he would be able to recognise Olivier Brusson as the one who had dragged the body away. Miossens replied, 'Apart from the fact that on that night the moon was shining brightly and I recognised the goldsmith perfectly well, I also saw at La Reynie's the dagger with which Cardillac was struck down. It's mine, distinguished by the delicate work on the handle. Standing only a step away from him, I could see every feature on the boy's face: his hat had fallen off, and of course I would be able to recognise him again.'

D'Andilly silently fixed his eyes on the floor before him for a few moments, then he said, 'Brusson is absolutely incapable of being rescued from the hands of justice by any of the usual channels. For Madelon's sake he will not name Cardillac as a thief and murderer. He can persist in his refusal, for even if he could succeed in proving Cardillac's guilt by showing the secret exit and the hoard of stolen treasure, he would still be executed as an accomplice. The result will be the same if Count Miossens discloses to the judges what really happened with the goldsmith. Postponement is the only thing we can hope for. Count Miossens must go to the Conciergerie, have himself presented to Olivier Brusson, and recognise him as the man who took Cardillac's body away. He must hurry to La Reynie and say, 'In the rue St-Honoré I saw a man struck down; I was standing right next to the body when another man leapt out, bent over the body, and when he found signs of life, hoisted him onto his shoulders and carried him away. I recognised Olivier Brusson as this man.' This declaration will provide an occasion for a further cross-examination of Brusson who will be brought to hear Count Miossens' evidence. This is enough for the threat of torture to be suspended, and further enquiries made. That will be the time to turn to the King himself. It is then up to your perspicacity, my lady, to do this as skilfully as you can! In my opinion, it would be a good idea to reveal the whole secret to the King. Through Count Miossens' declaration, Brusson's confessions will be corroborated – as they will be when Cardillac's house is secretly searched. None of this can form the basis for a judicial finding, but it may justify the King's decision, supported by his inner feeling which, where a judge must punish, can pronounce mercy.' Count Miossens carried out to the letter everything that d'Andilly had advised, and indeed it all turned out as the latter had foreseen.

Now it was a question of going to see the King, and this was the most difficult aspect, since he harboured such revulsion towards Brusson, whom alone he considered to be the dreadful robber and murderer who had for so long kept Paris in such a state of anguish and fear that, when even the slightest allusion to the notorious trial was made, he flew into a dreadful rage. Mme de Maintenon, true to her principle of never talking about unpleasant things to the King, rejected every attempt to communicate with her, and so Brusson's fate was placed entirely in the hands of Mlle de Scudéri. After long pondering, she rapidly came to a decision and just as rapidly carried it out. She put on a black dress of heavy silk, arrayed herself in Cardillac's precious jewellery, hung a long, black veil over it, and appeared in this guise in the rooms of Mme de Maintenon at a time when the King was present. The noble figure of this venerable lady in her solemn costume had a majesty that could not fail to awaken deep respect even among such loose-living people as are accustomed to pass their frivolous, carefree lives in the ante-rooms of palaces. They all withdrew, abashed, to let her pass, and when she made her entrance, the King himself stood up in great admiration and came forward to meet her. His eye was immediately caught by the sparkle of the precious diamonds on the necklace and bracelets, and he cried, 'By heaven, that is Cardillac's work!' And then, turning to Mme de Maintenon, he added with a graceful smile, 'See, Mme Marquise, how our beautiful bride is mourning for her bridegroom.'

'Ah, gracious lord,' interrupted Mlle de Scudéri, as if prolonging the jest, 'how could it be seemly in a mourning bride to wear such dazzling adornments? No, I had quite given up this goldsmith, and would no longer be sparing him a thought, were it not that the dreadful image of how he had been murdered close to my house sometimes appears before me.'

'What?' asked the King. 'What! Have you seen him, the poor devil?' Thereupon Mlle de Scudéri recounted briefly how chance had brought her to Cardillac's house (she still refrained from mentioning Brusson's involvement) at just the moment the murder had been discovered. She depicted the wild grief of Madelon, the deep impression made on her by that child of heaven, and the way she had saved the poor girl from the hands of Desgrais amid the approving cheers of the crowd. Arousing ever-increasing interest she began to recount the scenes with La Reynie – with Desgrais – with Olivier Brusson himself.

The King, swept away by the power and liveliness of Mlle de Scudéri's vivid and picturesque account, did not notice that it was the story of the hateful trial of Brusson, such a source of revulsion for him, that she was telling; he was unable to utter a word, and merely gave vent to his inner emotion by an occasional exclamation. Before he could gather his wits, quite dumbfounded by the extraordinary tale he was hearing and not yet able to get it all clear in his head, Mlle de Scudéri was already at his feet, begging for mercy for Olivier Brusson. 'What are you doing?' the King broke out, grasping her by both hands and motioning her to a seat. 'What are you doing, my lady! – You have given me a strange surprise! – That really is a dreadful story! – Who can vouch for the truth of Brusson's fantastic story?' To which Mlle de Scudéri replied: 'The statement made by Miossens – the investigation in Cardillac's house – an inner conviction – Ah! Madelon's virtuous heart that recognised a virtue matching hers in the unhappy Brusson!'

The King, about to make a retort, turned round on hearing a commotion at the door. Louvois, who had been working in the next room, was looking in with a worried expression on his face. The King stood up and left the room to follow Louvois. Both Mlle de Scudéri and Mme de Maintenon considered this interruption to be dangerous, for having once been taken by surprise the King might beware of falling into the same trap again.

But after a few minutes the King came back in, paced rapidly up and down a couple of times, then planted himself, hands behind his back, right in front of Mlle de Scudéri and said, without looking at her, in a low voice, 'I would really like to see your Madelon!' To which Mlle de Scudéri replied, 'O gracious lord, what a great, great happiness you are granting to the poor, unhappy child – ah, you need only make a sign and you will see the little creature at your feet.' And then she hastened over to the door, as fast as she could in her heavy clothes, and called through it that the King requested the presence of Madelon Cardillac; then she came back, weeping and sobbing with rapture and emotion. Mlle de Scudéri had foreseen this favour, and so brought Madelon with her, who had been waiting with the Marquise's chambermaid, a short petition in her hands that d'Andilly had composed for her. In a few moments she was lying speechless at the King's feet. Anguish – consternation – timid respect – love and pain – all made the boiling blood race more and more quickly through the poor girl's veins. Her cheeks were glowing bright crimson – her eyes were gleaming with tears like bright pearls which from time to time fell through her silken eyelashes onto her lovely lily-white breast.

The King seemed struck by the marvellous beauty of this angelic child. He gently raised Madelon to her feet, then made a movement as if he wanted to kiss her hand, which he had taken in his. He dropped it and looked at the fair child with a tear-moistened gaze that betrayed his deep inner emotion. Mme de Maintenon softly whispered to Mlle de Scudéri, 'Doesn't the young thing look just like La Vallière?[11] There's not a hair's difference between them! The King is indulging in his sweetest memories. Your game is won.'

Even though Mme de Maintenon had spoken quite quietly, the King seemed to have heard. A blush covered his face, his eyes flickered across Mme de Maintenon, he read the petition that Madelon had handed to him, and then he said gently and kindly, 'I am quite prepared to believe that you, my dear child, are convinced of your beloved's innocence, but let's hear what the *Chambre ardente* has to say about it!'

A gentle wave of his hand dismissed the girl, who was about to dissolve in tears. Mlle de Scudéri perceived with fright that this reminiscence of La Vallière, however advantageous it had been initially, had altered the King's intentions the minute

Mme de Maintenon had pronounced her name. Perhaps the King had been made aware – in a somewhat unsubtle way – that he was about to sacrifice strict justice to beauty, or perhaps he felt like the dreamer who, when his name is called, finds that the beautiful and magical images that he thought he was embracing quickly vanish. Perhaps he no longer saw his La Vallière before him, but was thinking only of Soeur Louise de la Miséricorde – the name La Vallière had taken when she took the veil in the Carmelites' convent – whose piety and penitence tormented him so much. Nothing else could be done other than quietly await the King's decision.

The statement made by Count Miossens to the *Chambre ardente* had meanwhile become widely known and, as it often happens that the populace is easily driven from one extreme to the other, so it was that the same man who had been cursed as the most vile murderer and threatened with a mobbing even before he could climb the scaffold was now pitied as the innocent victim of a barbaric justice. Now for the first time his neighbours remembered his virtuous ways, his great love for Madelon, and the loyalty, the devotion of body and soul that he had shown for the old goldsmith. – Whole crowds of people started to appear, looking menacing, outside La Reynie's palace and shouting, 'Bring Olivier Brusson out to us, he's innocent!' and even throwing stones at the windows so that La Reynie was obliged to seek police protection from the angry mob.

Several days went by without Mlle de Scudéri hearing even the slightest thing about Olivier Brusson's trial. Quite inconsolable, she went to see Mme de Maintenon, but the latter assured her that the King was saying nothing about the case, and it did not seem a good idea to remind him of it. When she asked with a strange smile what little La Vallière was doing,

Mlle de Scudéri persuaded herself that, deep within that proud woman, feelings of annoyance were stirring at the thought that the King might be lured into a territory whose magic she understood nothing of. She concluded that she could hope for nothing at all from Mme de Maintenon.

Finally with d'Andilly's help Mlle de Scudéri managed to find out that the King had had a long, private conversation with Count Miossens. She learnt further that Bontemps, the King's most intimate valet and chargé d'affaires, had been in the Conciergerie and spoken with Brusson, and that one night this same Bontemps had been with several people to Cardillac's house, staying there a long time. Claude Patru, who lived on the lower floor, assured them that there had been a commotion overhead all night long and that Olivier had certainly been involved, for he had clearly recognised his voice. This much was also certain, that the King himself was having the true chain of events investigated, but it was inconceivable why the result was taking so long to be made known. La Reynie was using all his resources to keep his prey gripped firmly between his teeth so as to prevent it being torn from him. This nipped every hope in the bud.

Nearly a month had gone by, when Mme de Maintenon had Mlle de Scudéri informed that the King wanted to see her in her, Maintenon's, apartment.

Mlle de Scudéri's heart leapt up; she knew that Brusson's case was now about to be decided. She told poor Madelon, who was fervently praying to the Virgin and all the saints, that only they could now awaken in the King the conviction of Brusson's innocence.

And yet it appeared that the King had forgotten the whole business for, just as before, lingering in graceful conversation with Mme de Maintenon and Mlle de Scudéri, he did not utter a single syllable about poor Brusson. Finally Bontemps appeared, approached the King and spoke a few words in such a low voice that neither of the ladies could hear. – Mlle de Scudéri was trembling within. Then the King stood up, went over to Mlle de Scudéri and said, with glittering eyes, 'I wish you happiness, my lady! – Your protégé, Olivier Brusson, is free!' Mlle de Scudéri, tears starting from her eyes, unable to utter a word, made to throw herself at the King's feet. He himself prevented her, saying: 'Come, come! My lady, you should be an advocate in parliament and fight my legal cases, for, by St Denis, no one on earth can resist your eloquence. – And yet,' he added gravely, 'and yet, he whom virtue itself takes under its protection may not always be safe from malicious accusations, from the *Chambre ardente* and all the lawcourts in the world!'

Mlle de Scudéri finally managed to find the words with which to pour out her most fervent thanks. The King interrupted her, telling her that in her house she herself could expect to find much more ardent thanks than he could expect from her, since at that very moment the happy Olivier was already doubtless embracing his Madelon. 'Bontemps,' concluded the King, 'Bontemps is to pay out a thousand louis d'or to you; give them in my name to the girl as a bridal present. If she then wishes to marry her Brusson, who does not deserve such a happiness, both of them must leave Paris. That is my will.'

Martinière came rushing up to Mlle de Scudéri, and behind her Baptiste, both their faces beaming with joy, both of them rejoicing and exclaiming, 'He's here! – he's free! – oh the dear young people!' The happy pair fell at Mlle de Scudéri's feet. 'Oh I knew all the time that you, you alone would save my bridegroom for me,' cried Madelon; 'Ah, my faith in you, my mother, was always steadfast in my soul,' cried Olivier, and both of them kissed the worthy lady's hands and shed a thousand hot tears. And then they embraced again and claimed that the more than earthly bliss of this moment made up for all the inexpressible sufferings of the past days; and they swore to stay with each other till death did them part.

A few days later they were joined together by the blessing of a priest. Even if it had not been the King's will, Brusson would not have been able to stay in Paris, where everything reminded him of the dreadful period of Cardillac's crimes, and where any chance event might lead to the disastrous revelation of the dark secret now known to several people and destroy his peaceful life for ever. Soon after the wedding he moved, accompanied by the blessings of Mlle de Scudéri, with his young wife to Geneva. Richly provided for, thanks to Madelon's bridal present, gifted with his unusual skill in the workshop, and with all the virtues of a good burgher, his life there turned out to be happy and carefree. In him were fulfilled the hopes that had been disappointed in his father and had driven him to his grave.

A year had gone by since Brusson's departure when a public declaration appeared, signed by Harlay de Champ-vallon, Archbishop of Paris, and the parliamentary advocate Pierre Arnaud d'Andilly, saying that a penitent sinner had handed over to the Church under the seal of confession a rich hoard of stolen jewels and gold. Anyone who, up to the end of the year 1680, had been robbed of a piece of jewellery, especially if it had involved an attack on the open streets, should report to d'Andilly, and would, if the description of the stolen jewels matched precisely one of the pieces found, and if there were no other doubt about the probity of the claim, be given his jewellery back. – Many who in Cardillac's list had been entered as not murdered but simply stunned by a punch found themselves turning up one by one at the house of the parliamentary advocate, and to their considerable astonishment got back the jewellery stolen from them. The rest fell to the treasury of St Eustache.

1. Madame de Maintenon was secretly married to Louis XIV in 1683; in 1680, Louis was still married to Marie-Thérèse of Austria.

2. Mlle de Scudéri's *Clélie* was in fact published in 1654–60.

3. The Hôtel-Dieu was a hospice for the poor and destitute. Hoffmann's account of the 'affaire des poisons' is fairly close to history.

4. The *Chambre ardente* was a tribunal notorious for its vigour that was set up in 1679 to try major criminals in the wake of the various poison scandals that had rocked Paris, as Hoffmann recounts.

5. 'A lover frightened of thieves / Is not worthy of love.' These words are attributed to Mlle de Scudéri.

6. Nicolas Boileau-Despréaux (1636–1711), a satirical poet and critic, was author of the famous '*Art poétique*'.

7. Chapelle (1626–86) was a satirical writer; Jean Racine (1639–99) a tragedian and historiographer; and Claude Perrault (1613–88) a doctor and designer of the new colonnade of the Louvre.

8. The Conciergerie was a notoriously harsh prison in central Paris.

9. The Trianon is a subsidiary palace within the grounds of Versailles.

10. 'The true may not always be credible' – the words are taken from Boileau's '*Art poétique*' (1674).

11. Louise-Françoise de La Vallière (1644–1710) became the mistress of Louis XIV while still in her teens, but eventually entered the Carmelite convent of the rue St-Jacques in the Latin Quarter.

Ernest Theodor Amadeus (originally Wilhelm) Hoffmann was born in Königsberg in 1776. From an early age he showed a great fascination for the arts, in particular music and painting, and he was noted for being a quick learner with a sharp intellect. He went on to study law, and held a number of legal positions with the Prussian civil service. Throughout his legal career, he maintained his passion for the arts, giving music lessons in his spare time. He eventually gave up the legal profession choosing instead to work as a music critic, director and conductor. By his thirties, however, he realised he would never become as great a composer as those he admired – in 1813 he had changed his name to Amadeus in homage to Mozart – and so turned to writing.

Following the publication of his first stories, Hoffmann soon became one of the most popular writers of his day. His works, notably *Nachtstücke* [*Night Pieces*] (1816), were some of the first of the modern 'horror' genre, in which he explored the nature of the grotesque and which had profound influence on many subsequent writers including Edgar Allan Poe, Robert Louis Stevenson and Franz Kafka. Perhaps inspired by his own struggles to reconcile his professional career with his creative aspirations, many of his characters had split personalities, honourable by day, murderers and thieves by night. His stories also formed the basis for a number of ballets, in particular Delibes's *Coppelia*, Tchaikovsky's *Nutcracker*, and Hindemith's *Cardillac*, and many were adapted for the theatre.

In later life, Hoffmann suffered from progressive paralysis and it was this that led to his death in 1822.

Andrew Brown studied at the University of Cambridge, where he taught French for many years. He now works as a freelance teacher and translator. He is the author of *Roland Barthes: the Figures of Writing* (OUP, 1993), and various translations of works relating to French history and philosophy.

HESPERUS PRESS – 100 PAGES

Hesperus Press, as suggested by the Latin motto, is committed to bringing near what is far – far both in space and time. Works written by the greatest authors, and unjustly neglected or simply little known in the English-speaking world, are made accessible through new translations and a completely fresh editorial approach. Through these short classic works, each little more than 100 pages in length, the reader will be introduced to the greatest writers from all times and all cultures.

For more information on Hesperus Press, please visit our website: **www.hesperuspress.com**

To place an order, please contact:
Grantham Book Services
Isaac Newton Way
Alma Park Industrial Estate
Grantham
Lincolnshire NG31 9SD
Tel: +44 (0) 1476 541080
Fax: +44 (0) 1476 541061
Email: orders@gbs.tbs-ltd.co.uk

SELECTED TITLES FROM HESPERUS PRESS

Gustave Flaubert *Memoirs of a Madman*

Alexander Pope *Scriblerus*

Ugo Foscolo *Last Letters of Jacopo Ortis*

Anton Chekhov *The Story of a Nobody*

Joseph von Eichendorff *Life of a Good-for-nothing*

Mark Twain *The Diary of Adam and Eve*

Giovanni Boccaccio *Life of Dante*

Victor Hugo *The Last Day of a Condemned Man*

Joseph Conrad *Heart of Darkness*

Edgar Allan Poe *Eureka*

Emile Zola *For a Night of Love*

Daniel Defoe *The King of Pirates*

Giacomo Leopardi *Thoughts*

Nikolai Gogol *The Squabble*

Franz Kafka *Metamorphosis*

Herman Melville *The Enchanted Isles*

Leonardo da Vinci *Prophecies*

Charles Baudelaire *On Wine and Hashish*

William Makepeace Thackeray *Rebecca and Rowena*

Wilkie Collins *Who Killed Zebedee?*

Theophile Gautier *The Jinx*

Charles Dickens *The Haunted House*

Luigi Pirandello *Loveless Love*

Fyodor Dostoevsky *Poor People*

Henry James *In the Cage*

Francesco Petrarch *My Secret Book*

André Gide *Theseus*

D.H. Lawrence *The Fox*

Percy Bysshe Shelley *Zastrozzi*

7. Feb. 04

Midwest 11-16 (12-20)

90511